W9-ABJ-948

"Logan!" she shrieked, arms folded over her head.

This time he was the one chuckling. "You ready to call a truce, little darlin'?" he asked as he shifted the hose's aim to the plants on the table beside her.

"Yes," she sputtered as she turned to face him. Water clung to the spiraling strands of her hair like a heavy morning dew. Coppery curls hung in sagging, wet tendrils to frame her pretty face.

A memory came rushing back from the past. One that had been very much like this moment. He and Hope in this very same greenhouse, both armed with hoses. Both soaked clean through by the end of their water play. Both falling in love. Or so he had thought.

Logan shut off the nozzle's spray and tossed it onto the ground beside him. "You can take it from here. I've got work to do." That said, he walked out of the greenhouse.

And away from the painful memories of her walking away from what they'd once had.

Kat Brookes is an award-winning author and past Romance Writers of America Golden Heart® Award finalist. She is married to her childhood sweetheart and has been blessed with two beautiful daughters. She loves writing stories that can both make you smile and touch your heart. Kat is represented by Michelle Grajkowski with 3 Seas Literary Agency. Read more about Kat and her upcoming releases at katbrookes.com. Email her at katbrookes@comcast.net. Facebook: Kat Brookes.

Books by Kat Brookes

Love Inspired

Texas Sweethearts

Her Texas Hero
His Holiday Matchmaker
Their Second Chance Love

Their
Second Chance
Love

Kat Brookes

HARLEQUIN® LOVE INSPIRED®

If you purchased this book without a cover you should be aware that this book is stolen property. It was reported as "unsold and destroyed" to the publisher, and neither the author nor the publisher has received any payment for this "stripped book."

Recycling programs
for this product may
not exist in your area.

 LOVE INSPIRED BOOKS

ISBN-13: 978-0-373-89925-8

Their Second Chance Love

Copyright © 2017 by Kimberly Duffy

All rights reserved. Except for use in any review, the reproduction or utilization of this work in whole or in part in any form by any electronic, mechanical or other means, now known or hereinafter invented, including xerography, photocopying and recording, or in any information storage or retrieval system, is forbidden without the written permission of the editorial office, Love Inspired Books, 195 Broadway, New York, NY 10007 U.S.A.

This is a work of fiction. Names, characters, places and incidents are either the product of the author's imagination or are used fictitiously, and any resemblance to actual persons, living or dead, business establishments, events or locales is entirely coincidental.

This edition published by arrangement with Love Inspired Books.

® and TM are trademarks of Love Inspired Books, used under license. Trademarks indicated with ® are registered in the United States Patent and Trademark Office, the Canadian Intellectual Property Office and in other countries.

www.Harlequin.com

Printed in U.S.A.

Love is patient, love is kind *and* is not jealous;
love does not brag *and* is not arrogant, does
not act unbecomingly; it does not seek its own,
is not provoked, does not take into account
a wrong *suffered*.
—*1 Corinthians* 13:4–5

I would like to dedicate this book
to my good friend Tammy Johnson,
who talked me into submitting to Love Inspired
after she sold her book to Love Inspired Suspense.
Without her pushing me to take the chance, this
book would not have been. I'd also like to thank
my wonderful agent, Michelle Grajkowski from
3 Seas Literary Agency, and my two writing
besties, Janice Lynn and Lisa Childs,
for believing in me and brainstorming ideas
with me for so many years.

Chapter One

Logan Cooper grimaced as his gaze moved over the crisp white wedding invitation he held in his hands. One embossed with two shiny gold hearts with flowers woven around them. The matching fancy gold script announcing the specifics for his brother's big day. A day filled with love and promises of happily-ever-after. But not all relationships had storybook endings. He knew that firsthand.

Nathan should know that, too.

A heavy sigh pushed past Logan's lips.

How could his big brother have forgotten the depth of heartache that eventually came with loving someone? Either through something as painfully final as death, as was his brother's case with his beloved wife, Isabel. Or by having the one who you love walk away, leaving your heart feeling as though it had just been trampled by a herd of stampeding cattle, as was the case with him and Hope.

Please, Lord, don't let my brother be making a mistake by risking his heart again.

It wasn't that Logan didn't like Alyssa. She was everything good in a woman. Kind and caring. Compassionate and patient. All of which Nathan had needed desperately in his life. She'd brought him back from the brink of the emotional desolation he'd fallen into after Isabel's death a little over two years before. Alyssa had even played a huge part in helping his brother find his way to the Lord again when no one else had been able to do so. But if something was to happen to her...

Logan shook the thought away. Nothing was going to happen to Alyssa. They wouldn't let it. Setting the invitation and the fancy reply card that came with it onto the kitchen counter, he grabbed his truck keys, slapped his cowboy hat onto his head and headed outside. He had an order at Hope's Garden to pick up.

Hope's Garden. The local nursery, owned and run by Jack Dillan, had been named for Jack's daughter, Hope, the girl Logan had once loved. He and Jack had been doing business together for years, despite the painful breakup that had gone on between Logan and Hope. Painful at

least for him, because you had to love someone to be able to feel the pain that comes with
losing them.

I don't love you. Hope's blurted-out declaration that day so long ago still rang in his
ears. How had he been so wrong about her?
About them? Shaking the ever-troubling past
from his mind, he climbed into his truck and
set off down the narrow dirt drive that fronted
the three-bedroom log cabin his brothers had
helped him build a few years before.

His gaze drifted upward as he peered out the
front windshield, taking in the billowy dark
clouds gathering in the morning sky above him.
He prayed the rain would hold off until he'd
picked up and delivered the trees he'd ordered
for a job he was finishing up. Thankfully, the
rain was expected to clear the area in a day or
so, and temperatures were supposed to move
up from the high fifties to the low seventies.

Thunder rumbled loudly in the distance as he
turned off the main road and drove through the
open gates of Hope's Garden. "Hold off just a
little longer," Logan pleaded, casting a glance
skyward. Loading and unloading trees in the
cold and wet made for a miserable day.

A large greenhouse sat off to the left of the
winding drive while rows of potted shrubs and

trees lined the land to his right. Up ahead, the building that housed the checkout counter, and various fertilizers and assorted plant food options, looked an even brighter white against the darkening backdrop of that morning's sky. To its right sat two more greenhouses, which held a large selection of potted annuals and perennials and thick, green ferns.

Parking near the entrance, Logan zipped up his jacket. raising its collar to protect himself against the bite of the spring wind gusting outside. Large drops of rain began to splatter across the windshield as he threw open the door, jumped down and made a sprint for the building's entrance.

So much for beating the storm.

He hoped Jack had a fresh pot of coffee going. He could use a cup and he knew Jack would gladly offer.

Despite the unexpected and painful breakup he'd gone through with Hope nine years before, he and Jack had remained close. His friend had been every bit as stunned by the breakup as Logan had been. He'd fully expected them to marry after college and start working on a family of their own. When that hadn't happened, Jack had given Logan a reason to get up every morning. He'd encouraged him to take what he'd learned while working for him at the nursery and start his own landscaping business.

Logan had taken the suggestion to heart, using his passion for trees and plants and flowers to build up a business that had taken root and had long since become one of the most sought-after landscaping service companies in the county. Logan would be the first to admit that he wouldn't be where he was today without the unwavering trust and faith Jack had placed in his ability to start a business of his very own.

"Hello!" he called out as he pulled the glass entry door closed behind him.

Country music blared from the back office.

Grinning, Logan called out a little louder, "What's a man gotta do to get some service around here?"

When Jack didn't reply, he shook his head with a chuckle. His friend really did need to consider having his hearing checked. They'd made jokes about it in the recent months, but, in all seriousness, how did he expect to hear his customers when they came in with the radio blasting the way it was?

Logan rounded the counter and made his way down the short hallway to Jack's office. One they had spent many a morning in before starting their workdays, talking over a cup of coffee and an occasional donut if Logan had time to run into town to pick some up for them on his way.

Reaching the office, he noticed the door had been left slightly ajar. The heady aroma of freshly brewed coffee drifted out into the hallway to join the music. Eager for a cup, Logan stepped into the room.

He'd no sooner opened his mouth to ask if his friend was trying to burst both of their eardrums with the radio cranked up so loud when his gaze dropped down from the vacant desk chair to the unmoving form on the floor beside the old oak desk.

"Jack!" Logan gasped, his gut twisting as he took in the sight of Hope's father lying motionless on the cool, hardwood floor a few feet away. The radio lay on its side next to him along with an upturned aloe plant and the clay pot and soil it had once been nestled in.

Dear Lord, please don't let Jack be gone.

The ringing of her cell phone had Hope Dillan stepping away from the filing cabinet where she'd been pulling several client files for the lunch meeting she had scheduled with the rest of Complete Solar Management's marketing team that afternoon. Reaching into her desk, she dug inside her purse for her phone, wondering if there had been a change in place or time for their meeting.

A glance at the screen displayed a number she wasn't familiar with. Bringing the phone to her ear, she said, "Hope Dillan speaking."

"Hope, it's Logan."

She froze, anxiety immediately filling her. How had he gotten her cell phone number? Surely, her daddy wouldn't have gone against her wishes and given it to him. Not after all these years. Years she'd spent doing everything she could to avoid crossing paths with Logan Cooper. Even changing her cell phone number, because Logan wasn't a quitter and she wasn't as strong as she'd like to be when it came to cutting all of her heartstrings where he was concerned.

Logan was the kind of man who, when he loved someone, did it with his whole heart. Even after she'd gone and broken it. If only things could have been different. If only God hadn't decided to shatter her dreams. *Their dreams.*

"This really isn't a good time," she managed, her eyes tearing up as she spoke the words. She prayed she sounded less affected by his unexpected call than she felt at that moment. Because she was anything but unaffected. Her furiously pounding heart was proof enough of that.

The last time they'd spoken had been after the tornado struck Braxton, taking with it his parents, his sister-in-law and their neighbor, Mr. Timmons. She'd returned home for the funerals.

How could she not? His family had been like her own.

"I had no choice," he said. There was no missing the unsteadiness to his voice.

"Logan, we—"

"This isn't about us," he said, cutting her off. "I'm calling about Jack."

"Daddy?" she said, her sense of panic shifting as his words settled in. "What about Daddy?" she demanded anxiously. She had just spoken with him the evening before and he had been his usual teasing self.

"He's had some sort of spell."

"What sort of spell?"

"I don't know," he said with a sigh. "I stopped by to pick up an order and found him on the floor in his office."

A sob caught in her throat.

"I'll know more once I get to the hospital," he said.

The hospital?

"The ambulance just left," he continued. "They're taking him to County General as we speak. I'm headed there as soon as I close up the nursery."

Hope shut her eyes, her phone clutched tightly in her hand. "Was he conscious?"

There was a brief hesitation on the other end

of the line before Logan replied, "Not when I found him. But he was when they were loading him into the ambulance. He told me not to bother you at work, but I thought you would wanna know."

"I appreciate your calling," she said, shaking as she grabbed her purse from the open drawer. Then pushing away from her desk, she shot to her feet. "I'll be there as soon as I can book a flight," she said with forced calm, trying to hold it together when inside she was on the verge of falling apart. She couldn't lose her daddy. He was all she had.

"Call when you get close to the hospital," Logan said flatly. "I'll make sure I'm gone before you get here."

His stiffly spoken words broke her heart, knowing she had made him this way. Distant, almost hard. Tears spilled down her cheeks. Before she could respond, before she could tell him there was no need to leave on her account, he was gone. The line every bit as empty as she felt inside.

Logan sat next to Jack's hospital bed, feeling helpless. A feeling that didn't sit well with him. There had to be something more he could do for his friend. Jack had given him his first job. Had taught him everything he knew about flowers and plants and trees. And after encouraging him to take his passion for those things and start his own landscaping business, Jack had gone so far as to loan Logan the money to start that business up. He had long since paid Jack back the money he'd lent him. His business, Cooper Landscaping, had taken firm root. He had no doubt that his company's success was due in large part to Jack Dillan's support and guidance over the years, as well as his brothers' bringing him in on several of their company's construction projects. If the businesses or home owners contracting work through Cooper Construction were in need of landscaping to go with their newly built homes or businesses, Logan's company was at the top of the recommended landscaper list his brothers provided to their clients. Being the only local landscaping company in the immediate area had no doubt helped, as well.

The steady hiss of oxygen being fed through the tube in Jack's nose had Logan's brow creasing in concern. He hated seeing his friend this way. Jack Dillan, at fifty-nine years of age, was still in his prime. He wasn't the kind of man to sit around having others do things for him. He was a doer, grumbling anytime someone fussed over him. Except when Verna Simms stopped by to bring him some of her homemade chicken soup because she'd heard that he was suffering from a bout of the sniffles. He didn't seem to mind the pretty widow and owner of Big Dogs, the local diner, coddling him. Not that Jack would ever admit to having a liking for the attention she paid to him. He was too set in his ways. But Logan knew better. Maybe he ought to give Verna a call. She'd have him back to his old self in no time. The thought of it brought a semblance of a smile to Logan's tightly pressed lips.

Closing his eyes, he prayed for the Lord to give Jack the strength to pull through this health crisis. It had been hard enough having to call Hope with the news that her daddy was in the hospital. Now he was going to have to stick around, despite preferring to be gone when Hope arrived. Jack had asked him to call and tell Hope he was under the weather in case she tried to reach him, sugarcoating the truth and leaving out the details, which Logan refused to do. Hope needed to know the whole of it. Dragging a hand back through his own dark, wavy hair, he took in Jack's pale face as he lay asleep in the hospital bed. "You'd best get to mending, old man. A lot of folks are gonna be counting on you for their garden flowers with spring being just around the corner." *He* was gonna be counting on Jack to be there.

His gaze flicked to the clock on the wall, watching as the second hand made its painfully slow trip around the circle of numbers. Over and over. Tick. Tick. Tick.

Unable to sit there listening to the hiss of the oxygen and the beeping of the monitors any longer, Logan pushed out of the hospital chair and straightened his six-foot-four-inch frame. Casting one more glance down at his friend, he turned and made his way out of ICU. He figured he'd return a few work calls that had come in that morning. Anything to fill the time and keep his concern at bay.

The automatic doors eased closed behind him as Logan stepped out into the hallway. Digging into the front pocket of his jeans, he grabbed for his cell phone and had just settled back against the brightly lit corridor's wall outside when a very feminine, all-too-familiar voice called out to him.

"Logan?"

His hand, still curled around his phone, dropped down to his side, his gaze shifting in the direction of the approaching hospital visitor. *Hope.* He stood frozen for a long moment, drinking in the sight of the woman he had once loved as she made her way toward him, wheeling a small floral suitcase behind her.

"Hope," he replied, shoving his cell phone back into his jeans pocket as he pushed away from the wall. Her wide green eyes were red-rimmed and swollen. Her normally beautiful, sun-kissed face void of color.

"I know I was supposed to call when I got in," she said, sounding panicked. "But my flight was delayed and all I could think about when we finally landed was getting here as quickly as I could."

"Your daddy's gonna be okay," he told her with less conviction than he'd like to have put across. *He had to be.* Hope needed him. *He* needed Jack, truth be told. The older man was like a second father to him.

Sniffling, she brushed away a stray tear that had started down her cheek. Then she looked up, searching his gaze. "Have you heard anything yet?"

Instinct had him wanting to reach out and comfort her. But it was better to keep his distance where Hope was concerned. He took a moment to collect his thoughts, to tuck away the emotions Hope never failed to stir in him. Hurt. Anger. Resentment. Longing.

"Logan," she said, the urgent plea pulling him from his troubled thoughts. "Please tell me."

He heaved a heavy sigh. "The doctor stopped

by to look in on your daddy about thirty minutes or so ago. He told us that the tests they'd run so far have confirmed that Jack suffered a stroke."

"A stroke?" Hope gasped, her hand flying to her mouth. She shook her head in denial, sending long, coppery curls bouncing over her slender shoulders. "That can't be. He's not old enough. He doesn't even smoke," she went on as denial took hold.

He nodded. "I know. They're still running a few more tests, but the doctor's pretty confident Jack's high blood pressure contributed to his having the stroke."

Confusion filled her green eyes. "But Daddy doesn't have high blood pressure."

He frowned, knowing that Jack had probably kept that information to himself to keep Hope from worrying over him.

Understanding dawned in her eyes as she took in his reaction to her words. "He does," she said, the words a mere whisper.

Logan nodded. "Yes."

"And *you* knew about it?" she said, more a statement than an actual question.

"Jack made mention of it a while back," he admitted.

"And you didn't think to call and let me know he was having health issues?"

"I didn't have your contact information," he said soberly. "The only reason I was able to reach you today was because I got your number from Jack's cell phone to make the call."

"Oh," she said, guilt lacing her tone. Her gaze dropped to the front of his shirt. "I'm sorry. None of this is your fault. I shouldn't have snapped at you that way."

"Don't apologize," he told her. "You're upset. It's understandable. We just have to keep in mind that this isn't about us."

"Agreed."

"Our focus needs to be on getting Jack back on his feet."

Her chin snapped up, her tear-filled eyes searching his. "So he really is gonna be all right?"

"He got to the hospital in time to put the odds back in his favor," he explained, repeating the doctor's earlier words.

"Thanks to you."

"Thanks to the Lord," he muttered. God had put him in the right place at the right time. "They need to get your daddy back on his medication, make adjustments as necessary to get his blood pressure under control. Once that's done, he should be his old self."

"Back on?"

"Apparently, Jack decided to stop taking his blood pressure medication about four months or so ago because he'd been feeling so well."

"Oh, Daddy," she groaned.

"There's a good possibility he's gonna require physical therapy of some sort, because he's experiencing some muscle weakness on one side, mostly with his arm. Barring any unforeseen issues, he should make a near, if not complete, recovery."

More tears sprung to her eyes. "I should get in there," she said, her gaze drifting to the double doors leading into ICU.

"I'll walk you back," he said as he reached for the handle of her suitcase. "Jack's in the first room on the left." If one could call the small, glass-enclosed cubicle where patients could be monitored visually as well as with machines a *room*.

"Is he conscious?" she asked fearfully.

"Yes," he answered with a nod as the ICU doors swung open. "However, he was sleeping when I stepped out here to return a few work calls."

"Did you tell him I was on my way?" she asked as they entered the intensive care unit.

"He doesn't know that you're aware he's in here," he said evenly. "He didn't wanna cause you any worry."

"I'm glad you called," she said. "Not that Daddy will be, I'm sure. The man's too proud for his own good."

Logan gave a shrug. "I did what needed done. He'll get over it." Jack had never been a man to hold grudges.

Hope stopped just outside the cubicle, staring at her daddy through the floor-to-ceiling wall of windows. "He looks so helpless. He's never been helpless," she said, biting at her bottom lip.

Logan stepped up beside her, his gaze focused on the man beyond the glass. "Don't worry. You know Jack's got more grit in him than most men I know. You've just gotta trust in the Lord to watch over him."

"Where was *the Lord* when Daddy had his stroke?"

She sounded so bitter. Not at all like the Hope that he used to know. But the woman he'd thought he'd once known was little more than a stranger to him now. She'd seen to that.

"*He* was there," he assured her. "I know it's hard to see your daddy all hooked up to wires and tubes, but you've gotta stay strong for his sake," he told her, resisting the urge to reach for her hand as he would have done back when they were a couple. Back when he was a naive teenage boy who thought he knew what true love was.

He watched as she shored up her slender shoulders. No doubt gathering the emotional courage to step into the room, into the reality of the situation she found herself in.

Logan followed, wheeling her suitcase up against the glass wall by the entrance where he stood waiting, giving Hope a moment of privacy as she moved to stand beside Jack's hospital bed.

Reaching for Jack's limp hand, Hope covered it with her own. "Oh, Daddy," she said as her worried gaze took in the medical equipment that surrounded the head of his hospital bed. Leaning over the bed rail, she said softly, "Daddy, it's Hope. Can you hear me?"

He stirred, his lashes lifting slightly as he peered up at his only child. "Baby girl?" he said, his thick brows furrowing in confusion.

She managed a bright smile, as she settled into the chair next to the bed rail. "You gave me a scare."

"What are you doing here?" he asked in surprise.

"I wouldn't be anywhere else."

"But how did you know I was…" His words trailed off as his tired gaze shifted to where Logan stood waiting. One lone salt-and-pepper brow lifted. "You called her?"

He nodded. Not that he'd wanted to. "She had a right to know."

"Not one for sticking to the plan, I see," Jack grumbled.

"No, sir," Logan replied with a shake of his head as he stepped closer. "Not when it means keeping something this serious from your daughter." No matter how poorly things had ended between the two of them, he knew what it was like to lose a parent. Hope had already lost her momma. If Jack, God forbid, took a turn for the worse, she deserved the chance to say goodbye. Even if she had pretty much abandoned Jack when she'd moved away, her visits too few and far too short. Jack deserved more from his only child.

"I see," his friend said with clear disapproval.

Betraying Jack wasn't something Logan had done lightly. But his momma had raised him to do the right thing. This, in his opinion, had been the right thing to do, whether Jack liked it or not. "I'd do it again if the situation called for it," he admitted.

Hope turned her head, looking up at him. "And I thank you. I'm sure it wasn't an easy call to make, seeing as how Daddy asked you to keep this to yourself."

She had no idea how difficult. Not only because of the news he'd had to give her, but also because hearing her sweet voice again had succeeded in twisting him up in emotional knots all over again. It had also stirred up the bitterness and hurt he'd long since tucked away.

"If not for your finding Daddy…" she continued, emotion drawing her voice tight.

"Yes," Jack agreed with a nod. "If you hadn't been there… Thank you, son. For everything."

"Don't thank me," he told the older man with a smile. "Thank the man above. Appears He's still got plans for you."

"Appears that way."

"Well, now that you've got family here, I'll be on my way," he said, needing to put some distance between himself and Hope. Pulling Jack's smartphone from the front pocket of his flannel shirt, Logan placed it atop the narrow lap table that hovered over the foot of Jack's hospital bed. "In case you need to reach me. Take care of yourself, Jack. I'll be by tomorrow to check on you." Looking to Jack's daughter, he tipped his hat. "Hope." Then turning, he made his way toward the open doorway.

"Logan," Jack called after him, his voice weak.

He stopped then turned to find knowing eyes watching him.

"Everything will work itself out, son. The good Lord's got plans for you, as well."

He didn't miss Hope stiffening at her daddy's words of faith in the Lord. Just as she had earlier.

He acknowledged Jack's words with another nod and then walked out of the ICU room. Back to what he knew best—landscaping.

But when his thoughts should have turned to that day's business, they stubbornly refused. They were caught up in the change he'd seen in Hope. She wasn't the sweet, smiling girl he remembered. The one he'd spent countless Sundays sitting beside in church all those years ago. The one he'd laughed with. Learned with. Loved. No, the woman he'd seen today had lost that spark of joy that used to light her green eyes. Even more troubling, she seemed to have lost her trust in God's will.

He sighed, wishing he could push the troubling thoughts away. Getting caught up in Hope again wasn't something he would ever allow to happen. But it didn't mean he wasn't affected by her rejection of a faith she'd once held dear.

Granted, there had been a time when her trust in the Lord had been shaken. Right after her momma had lost her long, courageous battle with cancer. But she'd been young and scared and hurting. His momma, who had been close with Hope's, had done her best to step in and help fill in some of the void. She'd also been

there to help an eleven-year-old little girl understand and accept that the Lord had a far greater
plan for her momma.

Now he had to wonder if Hope had ever really accepted that. Had she merely put on a front
about having faith all these years just as his
own brother had done after the loss of his wife?
Logan couldn't even begin to guess what was
going on inside her head. He'd already been so
wrong about so many things where Hope Dillan was concerned. Best thing for him to do was
keep his distance.

Hope watched him go, tears pooling up in
her eyes. Logan Cooper was no longer the boy
that she had fallen in love with all those years
ago. He was a full-grown man. Tall, lean, broad-
shouldered and with an even greater ability
to make her heart pound. He was everything
she had always dreamed about. Everything she
could ever hope for. Not that it mattered. She
had lost him long ago.

Frowning, she turned back to her daddy, who
was watching her, his tightly pressed lips pulling downward. "Are you hurting?" she asked
worriedly, forcing all thoughts of Logan Cooper
from her mind.

"I'm thinking I should be asking you that
question," her daddy said.

She forced a smile. "I'm not the one lying in a hospital bed. Now stop worrying yourself over me."

"No can do, honey," he replied. "You're my baby girl. It's my job to worry over you."

"Well, there isn't anything to be concerned about," she said, wondering if she was trying to convince her daddy or herself. Seeing Logan again, talking to him again, being so near to him, had left her thoroughly shaken. Pushing thoughts of him from her mind, she said, "And it's *my* turn to worry about you. Not the other way around." Standing, she reached out to dim the light over the hospital bed. "Now get some rest. We can talk more later."

Jack nodded, his heavy-lidded eyes drifting shut.

Hope sat watching him for a long time, knowing how close she had come to losing him. The thought of no longer having him in her life had shaken her to the core. The Lord had already taken her mother away. A hurt that had only deepened when she'd learned she would probably never be a mother herself.

As it had so many times over the past nine years, a deep ache filled her at the thought. Her hand moved to smooth over her flat stomach, unshed tears filling her eyes. It would never grow round with a child. She would never feel the stirrings of life that came with carrying a baby of her own. Never find the true happiness she'd come so close to having before her life as she had known it came crashing down around her.

Chapter Two

"Logan?" his brother said, concern knitting his brows as he studied Logan from across the door's threshold. Boone, the bloodhound mix Carter had adopted from the pound for Audra's children, stood faithfully at his side.

"I know it's late," Logan began apologetically as he reached down to give the dog a scruff behind his ear.

"It's never too late for family," Carter countered. "Come on in." He stepped aside, Boone moving with him as he swung the front porch door open wider.

Removing his cowboy hat, Logan made his way inside, his gaze sweeping the entryway of the old farmhouse his brother's wife had purchased when she'd moved to Texas from Chicago with her two young children. Carter, who co-owned Cooper Construction with their brother, Nathan, had helped Audra with renovations on her house and the two had ended up falling in love. Now married and on the verge of adding to their already existent brood, Carter was happier than Logan had ever seen him.

"Audra in bed already?" Logan asked with a glance toward the stairs. He knew the children would be for sure. They both had school in the morning.

"Not yet," his brother replied. "She's in the kitchen cleaning up after the finger painting session she had with our little artists in the making after dinner. Who knew my wife was such a messy finger painter?"

"Maybe Alyssa could give her finger painting lessons," he suggested with a grin. Their oldest brother Nathan's fiancée had a degree in interior design and had taught art classes to children at the rec center where she used to live while working part-time for an interior design firm. Not wanting to be so far away from his brother and his little girl, Katie, Alyssa had left the life she had built for herself in San Antonio and was now teaching art classes on weekends at Braxton's newly built recreation center. She was also in charge of interior design for any of Cooper Construction's projects that called for it.

His brother nodded. "Might have to consider that."

Logan cast a glance toward the front door. He really should go. Not stick around to lay his problems at his brother's feet. Carter already had his plate full with a new wife, helping to raise her two beautiful children, whom he'd recently adopted, and a baby on the way.

"I know that look."

He looked back at his brother. "What look?"

"The one that says you're considering making a run for the hills," Carter replied.

When they were teens and something upset them, one or all of them would take to the hills where they'd hike and camp and work through whatever it was that was bothering them. There was just something about the peace and tranquility of being surrounded by nature, not to mention the feeling of being closer to God that being higher up in the hills gave a man. But when it came to his troubled thoughts where Hope was concerned, there would be no answers.

"I feel like it," he answered honestly. If he thought it would help to clear his head, he'd be driving up into the hills right now. Instead, he'd come seeking his brother's counsel.

"So what's up?"

"Jack's in the hospital," he said with a heavy sigh, struggling to keep the tide of emotion from washing over him.

Concern immediately lit Carter's eyes. Understandably so. They were all close with Jack Dillan. "What happened?"

Logan dragged a hand back through the thick waves of his hair. "He suffered a stroke at work this morning. I found him on the floor of his office when I stopped by to pick up an order."

"Why didn't you call? Nathan and I would have met you at the hospital."

"I knew you were finishing up a job in the next town over," he explained. "Figured I'd wait until we had some answers."

"No wonder you're not yourself," his brother replied. "Is he gonna be okay?"

"He's got a long road ahead of him until he's fully recovered, but the good Lord's seen fit to give Jack more time here on this earth."

"Praise God for that," his brother muttered. "Does Hope know yet?"

Logan nodded. "I called to let her know what had happened as soon as the ambulance pulled away with Jack. She caught the first flight out of San Diego and managed to get to the hospital a little after four."

Carter's assessing gaze studied him. "So you've seen her, then?"

"I was there when she arrived."

"That also explains this mood that you're in," his brother acknowledged.

"It's not what you think."

"That she refused to enter the hospital until you left?" his brother surmised, not bothering to hide his irritation where Hope was concerned. "Because that's what I expect happened."

Nathan and Carter were none too happy with Hope for the way she had handled the postbreakup with their younger brother. With the exception of the tearful embrace she had given him at his parents' and Isabel's funerals, her intentional avoidance of Logan and the scant number of times she could drag herself back to Braxton to visit Jack had his brothers harboring more than a little resentment toward her.

Then again, Logan harbored his own fair share of that same emotion where Hope Dillan was concerned.

"It didn't happen like that," he heard himself saying in Hope's defense. Though why he felt the need to stick up for her was beyond him.

"So you left before she got there?"

He probably should have. Then he wouldn't be struggling over thoughts of the past and feeling things he'd spent years suppressing. But Hope had looked so lost when he'd looked up to see her standing in that hospital corridor. All he'd wanted to do at that moment was comfort her. Thankfully, he hadn't followed through with what instinct had been pushing him to do. It would have undoubtedly ended up with her pushing him away—again. And he'd had more than his fill of Hope rejecting him.

"Neither of us ran," Logan muttered as he stood fingering the brim of his hat. "We were both there for Jack. It had nothing to do with us." That was how it had to be, because there was no "us" when it came to him and Hope.

Carter nodded. "I'll be sure to say an extra prayer tonight asking for the Lord to help ease your way while Hope's home." He reached out to clap a hand over Logan's shoulder, giving it a supportive squeeze. "Come on in to the kitchen with me and we'll have us a cup of coffee."

"I really should be going. It's been a long day."

"Audra made pecan pie…"

Logan hesitated a long moment before a smile quirked his lips. "Pecan pie, huh?"

"Complete with a scoop of vanilla ice cream and caramel syrup," his brother tempted even further, knowing Logan had the biggest sweet tooth of any of the Cooper boys.

Maybe he would stay. Just for a bit. And by the time he finished with his coffee and dessert he'd have his emotions, as far as Hope Dillan was concerned, corralled once more. Because there was no way he was gonna risk putting his heart on the line ever again. Not for Hope. Not for any woman.

* * *

Hope was startled awake by the familiar tune of "Take Me Home, Country Roads." She sat upright in the chair next to her dad's hospital bed. A quick glance assured the phone's ringtone hadn't awakened him as it had her. Hurriedly, she snatched the phone out of her purse, bringing it to her ear as she got to her feet and hurried from the cubicle. "Hello?" she answered in a hushed tone.

"Wasn't sure you'd answer," a voice far huskier than it had once been said at the other end of the line.

"Logan?" she said somewhat groggily.

A groan sounded. "I woke you."

"I was only catnapping."

"You probably needed it," he replied. "Getting news like you got today tends to take a toll on a person. I'm sorry I woke you. Go back to bed."

"Don't apologize," she said. "My back and neck thank you for waking me. But I'm not home. I'm still at the hospital. I guess I drifted off in the chair by Daddy's hospital bed in a rather uncomfortable position."

"How is Jack?"

"He's doing well," she replied, keeping her voice low as she stepped out of ICU and made her way to the family waiting area just around the corner. There she would be able to talk without waking her daddy, or disturbing the other patients. "If all goes well tonight, they'll be moving him to a private room tomorrow."

"Thank the Lord for that," Logan breathed, his relief, as well as the faith he steadfastly clung to, evident in his voice. A faith she herself no longer looked to when times were bad. "I'm sorry to bother you on your cell phone again, but when I tried Jack's it went straight to voice mail. I forgot that I had shut his phone off after calling you this morning."

"You added my number to your contact list?"

"No. I would never presume to do that. It's in my head," he explained.

"You still have a knack for remembering things others would more easily forget," she said with a wistful smile.

"You don't have to worry about my calling you after you've gone back to California. For now, if need be, I know I'll be able to reach you. The reason I called was to let Jack know that I'm gonna swing by Hope's Garden on my way home from Carter's to check on things. I didn't want either of you to worry yourselves over it tonight."

She started to tell him that his call wasn't a bother, then decided it best that he believed that it was. Especially because the sound of his voice was something she could get far too used to hearing. So caught up in her thoughts of keeping a wall up with Logan, it took a moment longer than it should have for what he'd said to settle in. Hope shifted the cell to her other ear. "You don't have to do that."

"I don't mind."

He had already done more than enough for her daddy. Now that she was home, it was her responsibility to step in and see to things until he was back on his feet again. "I know you don't," she said. "But as soon as I can round up a taxi, I'll be able to head home and see to those things myself."

"A taxi?"

How else did he expect her to get home? "While I could probably make the walk from here to Braxton, it might take a while, and doing so in the dark and in the pouring rain might be pushing it."

A warm chuckle sounded at the other end of the line. "You've been living in the big city for a mite too long, little darlin', if you think you're gonna round up a taxi around these parts, with the exception of the airport, with any ease," he said with an amused chuckle. "That'd be like trying to find an ocean of in the middle of the Sahara Desert."

Those two words wrapped around her, making her heart ache—*little darlin'*. She had to wonder if Logan even realized that he'd called her that. The nickname he'd given her back in high school when he'd first started working for her daddy at Hope's Garden. Not that she was all that little at five-foot six-inches tall. But to a boy well over six feet in height back then, and to the even taller man he'd grown up into, it was easy to see why Logan considered her *little*. But she was no longer his *darlin'*. No matter what her heart still longed for.

"I hadn't given it much thought," she answered honestly. Not with her focus centered for the most part on her daddy and the long road to recovery it sounded like he was going to have ahead of him.

"No, I suppose you wouldn't," came his muttered reply on the other end of the line.

What exactly did Logan mean by that? She opened her mouth to ask and then closed it, deciding it best to let it go. He had every right to be angry with her. Truth was she was surprised he'd been as cordial as he had been, considering how she'd ended things between them.

Logan wasn't one to quit on those he cared about, and if things were different, they'd more than likely be married with a few little ones running around. But things weren't different. And she'd had to break his heart to ensure he'd have those Cooper sons and daughters he'd always longed for.

"Hope? You still there?"

His voice pulled her back to the present. "Yes. I'm here."

"Thought maybe we got cut off there for a second. Phone service can be iffy inside hospitals."

She didn't correct his assumption. It was better he think her silence was due to phone service issues rather than her troubled thoughts.

"If you're ready to head back to your daddy's place," Logan said, saving her the need for any response, "I could run on over to Coopersville and pick you up. Then we can see to the nursery together before I head home for the night. I left in such an all-fire hurry this morning once the ambulance had gone, I didn't shut the register down or see to the plants."

"I would have done the same thing. And thanks for the offer, but I'll give Autumn a call to come get me."

"Still doing your best to avoid me, I see," he said evenly.

"I think we're beyond that now," she said, wishing it were true. But avoiding Logan kept her heart from wanting things she couldn't have. From wanting *him*. "Besides, I wanted to let Autumn know about Daddy and maybe do some catching up."

Autumn and Summer Myers, Braxton's only claim to identical twins, had been her closest friends all through school. After high school graduation, they'd all gone off to different colleges. And with everything that had been going on in her life at that time, the breakup with Logan, dealing with health issues and her anger with God, Hope had withdrawn from everyone she'd been close to, even her dearest friends.

"If you're counting on Autumn to come get you, you might be in for a long wait," he told her. "She's in Atlanta for some sort of Realtor conference this week."

How did he know that? A heart-pinching thought passed through her mind. *Were the two of them seeing each other?* It wasn't as if she expected Logan to spend the rest of his life pining away after her. She ended their relationship just so he could make his life with someone else. He deserved someone who could give him children. That would make him happy. Still, the thought of her best friend and the man Hope had given her heart to being romantically involved sat like a boulder in the pit of her stomach.

"Oh," was all she could manage. She should have thought to have the taxi she'd taken from the airport drop her off at home first. Then she could have driven her daddy's truck into Coopersville. But she'd been in such a panic that all she'd wanted to do from the moment her flight landed was get there to see for herself that he was all right.

A heavy sigh sounded at the other end of the line. "I'll come get you."

"No," she blurted out in a panic. "I mean, don't worry about me. I've got my suitcase with me. I'll just spend the night here."

"And how do you plan on getting home tomorrow?"

Hope frowned. That was a good question. There was no one else she could think to call. She had pretty much cut everyone she'd known growing up out of her life.

"I can leave the past in the past where it belongs if that's what you're worried about," Logan said.

"Why are you doing this?" she replied, her guilt at what she'd done to him all those years ago pushing to the surface. "Offering to give me a ride when you of all people should wanna stay as far away from me as possible." Her words ended on a quiver as she fought the urge to cry over his unexpected kindness.

"The easiest answer would be that I'm doing my Christian duty. But that wouldn't be the whole truth of it," he answered honestly. "I'm also doing it for Jack. He needs to focus on getting better, not focus his strength on worrying about you. Which, I might add, your daddy's done every single day of his life since you moved away."

He had? The guilt was swallowing her whole. "He doesn't need to worry about me."

"People tend to do that when they care about someone."

His tone hinted that she wouldn't understand that level of caring. She did. She had cared enough to let Logan go. Loved him enough to set him free to find the happiness he deserved. But then he wouldn't know that. "I'm sorry I hurt you."

A long silence fell over the line before Logan responded. "I'm sorry for not accepting your decision to end things between us," he said. "I should've respected your wishes and let you go. But I was young and had a lot of false notions about what my future held for me. For us."

"Logan…" she said, wanting to tell him that she'd wanted all the same things he had. Instead she fell silent. She couldn't offer up any explanation that would make him understand. It was too late.

"Let me finish," he told her. "What we had was special, but I know now that we were too young to be talking about marriage and kids. At least one of us had the sense to see that and do something about it. And you can stop worrying about being in the same room as me every time you come home, because I've come to terms with the fact that some things are just not meant to be."

Like her having children. A warm trail of tears ran down her cheeks. That was hard enough to deal with, but to hear Logan spell it out so clearly. To hear it straight from him that he had gotten over her, over them, over all the hopes and dreams they had once shared for their future, that it had simply been nothing more than youthful imaginings, was almost unbearable. It had been so much more.

She swallowed the knot of emotion building in her throat. *Stop being the fool, Hope Dillan. This is the way you wanted it to be. Needed it to be.*

Pulling herself together, as she'd had to do so many times in her life, she replied, "If you're sure it's no trouble, I'd like to take you up on your offer to give me a ride home."

"No trouble," he assured her. "When would you like me to pick you up?"

"Would now be too soon?" she asked hesitantly. "Daddy's finally sleeping comfortably and I need to get settled in at the house for my stay here."

"Now works for me. I'm on my way."

When the call disconnected, Hope brought the phone to her chest and closed her eyes. She could do this. It was only for a short time. Until her daddy got back on his feet and she could go back to the life she'd built for herself back in San Diego. Knowing that Logan had finally gotten over her helped to ease some of her guilt, even if it made her heart ache more.

Now all she had to do was keep a tight rein on her feelings for him. At the very least, keep them from being known, because she was still not the woman he needed in his life. One who could give him the future he'd always dreamed about.

There's a good possibility you may never be able to conceive. She'd never forget those words, so gently given to her by her doctor when she was only a senior in high school, a young girl filled with hopes and dreams for her future. One with Logan. The endometriosis she'd been diagnosed with during her sophomore year had worsened, causing a buildup of scar tissue in her fallopian tubes that without surgery would more than likely cause infertility. But even with surgery, the risk of having a tubal pregnancy was greatly increased.

She'd seen what her momma and daddy had gone through after trying for another child only to see both pregnancies end in miscarriages because of the severity of her mother's endometriosis. They'd been devastated.

She couldn't do that to Logan. To herself. So at eighteen, with no mother to guide her, she'd made the only decision she'd been emotionally capable of making at the time. She walked away from her dreams.

Gone was the deep faith she had once held dear. How was she supposed to continue clinging to that faith when God had taken so much from her? First her mother and then her own ability to become a mother herself.

She and Logan had shared so many things. A love of family, a passion for the outdoors and the dream of someday marrying and having a handful of children of their own to raise.

Then that life-altering diagnosis changed everything and brought her perfect world crashing down around her. She would never be able to give Logan the children he deserved to have.

She had always been honest with Logan, but this was the one thing she could never share with him. If he learned the truth, she knew he would have given up his dreams for her sake.

So she kept the heart-wrenching news she'd gotten at the doctor's that day so long ago to herself. Then she'd forced Logan out of her life by telling him she didn't want to be tied down by a relationship when they went off to college.

Only Logan had been determined not to give up on what they'd had together, making everything so much harder for them both.

So she'd taken extreme measures—she'd lied to him. Told him that she didn't love him. Not the way he wanted her to. Then she made it clear that he was wasting his time. To stop wishing for something that could never be. And then, with her heart breaking, she'd walked out of his life.

And now Logan was back in her life along with all those old feelings she'd tried so hard to shut off. But the damage was already done. Logan was only in her life again because of her daddy, nothing more.

Logan pulled up under the hospital overhang and threw his truck into Park. He was just rounding the front of the truck when Hope stepped through the hospital doors.

"Sorry I'm late," he said. "Had to take a different route due to some light flooding on the main road." Not a complete surprise seeing how much rain they'd gotten that day. And it was still coming down.

"I'm glad you didn't try going through it," she said as he swung open the passenger door and reached for the suitcase she had wheeled out behind her.

"I grew up here, remember?" he said as he took hold of the bag and lifted it into the truck, placing it just behind the front bench seat. "I know better." Flash floods, no matter how passable the water on the road might appear, could easily sweep a vehicle away. They were even more dangerous this time of year when floods weren't prevalent. Folks tended to be far less cautious.

As soon as Hope had settled herself in the passenger seat, Logan closed the door and then jogged around to his side of the truck. "Jack still sleeping?"

"He woke up right after I talked to you. I debated leaving him, but he insisted I go home and get some rest. He also added that he was counting on me to run things while he was incapacitated." That last part had her mouth turning downward.

He studied her from across the truck's dark cab, the glow of the hospital entrance lights illuminating her pretty face. "That could be a while," he said softly.

She nodded. "I know."

"Does Jack?"

"You know Daddy," she said. "He doesn't let much keep him down for long. He's already chomping at the bit to get back to the nursery."

"Being away from there for any amount of time has got to be real hard on him," Logan agreed. Working at the nursery day in and day out helped to keep the older man's loneliness at bay. Jack had admitted as much to Logan one morning over coffee not long after one of Hope's rare visits home. Logan understood. Putting his time and energy into his landscaping business left far less time to dwell on his own loneliness.

"It'll drive him crazy," Hope said, bringing Logan back to the present. "I'm hoping that not only will it motivate Daddy to think twice next time before taking himself off his prescribed medication, but that it will also push him to work hard in therapy so he can get back to doing what he loves. In the meantime, I'll be staying in Braxton to see that he does just that and to see to the running of the nursery."

Jack's recovery could take weeks, months even, before he was physically back to the point he was at prior to his stroke. That meant there would be no avoiding seeing Hope again and again. Was he ready for that? Not that it mattered, he decided. It was what it was.

"Won't they miss you at work?" he asked, hoping that maybe, just maybe, she hadn't thought things out completely and would need to get back to San Diego sooner rather than later.

"I've got vacation time as well as personal

time built up that I can use during my stay here. If I need more, I'll just take time off without pay," she told him. "Hopefully, I can remember everything Daddy taught me about running the nursery. It's been a while."

"Just like riding a bike," Logan said as he pulled out onto the main street. "I can lend you a hand for the next couple of weeks," he said without thinking. The last thing he wanted to do was spend time doing something that would bring back memories he'd just as soon forget. Memories of when he'd first started working at Hope's Garden for Jack and the time he'd spent getting to know Hope as the two of them worked side by side. Laughing together. Sharing hopes and dreams. Their first kiss.

"You have your own business to see to," she countered, her response giving him the out he needed.

He nodded. "I do. But I just had a landscaping job that was scheduled for next week get pushed back to early April," Logan heard himself offering, despite his reservations. He was doing this for Jack. Putting his issues with Hope aside for his friend's sake. "I can help cover for you while your daddy's in the hospital. That'll free you up to spend more time with him while he's there. Once he comes home, we can take turns looking after him and the nursery."

"I should refuse your offer," she said, glancing his way.

"But you won't," he said knowingly.

"I can't," she answered honestly. "But I wanna pay you for your time."

He shook his head, his gaze fixed on the road ahead. "Not gonna happen. Jack's my friend. I'm offering to lend a hand because of that."

"You win," Hope said with a sigh. "I have to focus on getting Daddy better right now. So whatever it takes, I'm willing to do it."

He hadn't won. If he had, the past nine years would have been a whole lot different. And winning wasn't having a woman agree to keep you underfoot because she didn't have any other choice.

He'd known when he'd made the offer that Hope would be a hard sell. Even Carter had tried to talk him out of spending any more time with her than he had to. But his momma raised him to be a good Christian. To help those in need. Just as his brother had helped Audra when she'd first arrived in Braxton.

Only in Logan's case, there would be no happy ending. As soon as Jack recovered, Hope would return to the life she'd built for herself in San Diego. And he'd be left dealing with questions he knew going in that he'd never have the answers to.

"Logan…"

He glanced her way.

"I never really had the chance to tell you during the funeral services how very heartbroken I was over the loss of your momma and daddy. And Isabel, as well."

That was because Hope had been in such an all-fire hurry to put distance between himself and her. There had been a quick hug followed by a teary-eyed "take care of yourself," and then she was gone.

"You came," he told her, his gaze returning to the road ahead. "That's all that mattered. Momma would have been touched that you made the trip home for her service."

"I loved her," she said sadly, and he didn't doubt her words in the least.

His momma had done her best to fill in for the friend she had lost far too soon, taking eleven-year-old Hope with her to teas and shopping and to get her hair done. All those things a mother and daughter would have done together. His momma had done those things, not only because of the love she'd had for the friend she'd lost, but because she'd just plain enjoyed spending time with Hope. She'd never had any daughters of her own to share those special moments with. Just three big, strapping boys who preferred camping, riding horses and long hikes in the woods.

"I loved both of your parents," Hope added with a sniffle.

"I know you did." It was him she couldn't find it in her to love.

Silence fell between them the rest of the way to Hope's Garden. The only sound came from the purr of the truck's engine and the rhythmic swish of the windshield wipers as they pushed away the heavy rain.

When they turned onto the road that led to the nursery and Jack's place just beyond, Hope sat up, her attention focused on the building ahead. "There are lights on in the office," she said worriedly.

"I know," he said, pulling up in front of the brightly lit building. Its warm glow filtered into the cab of the truck. "I was in such a hurry to get to the hospital this morning after the ambulance took Jack away that I forgot to shut them off. I did, however, remember to hang the Closed sign on the door and lock up before I left." Cutting the engine, he undid his seat belt and reached into the front pocket of his jeans, pulling out Jack's key ring. "You'll be needing these."

"He still has this?" she said, a bit misty-eyed as she ran her fingers over the pink daisy key ring, the colorful paint long since worn away along its edges. She lifted her gaze to meet his. "I gave him this for Christmas when I was in eighth grade."

Logan eyed the key-laden piece. "Reckon it meant a lot to him for him to still be carrying it around."

She laughed softly. "I probably should've bought him a cowboy boot key chain or something a little more manly. But I was big on flowers and anything and everything pink back then. I remember drawing pink flowers all over my school folders."

"Back then?" he said with a snort as he reached for the handle on the driver's door panel. "It went well beyond eighth grade. I seem to recall you doodling flowers all over my book covers when we were in high school." His gaze shifted her way to find Hope biting back a grin. "Funny to you, little darlin'," he said with a grin of his own. "Not so funny when you're a teenage boy wanting to come across as rough and tough on the football field and your teammates are calling you 'Pretty Posey Cooper.'"

A giggle erupted from her lips. "You never told me that."

"And make myself come across as less than manly in your eyes as well as my teammates? Not a chance."

"Oh, Logan, I'm sorry."

"They were only having fun with me," he replied. "Truth be told, it improved my game. In an effort to prove myself more than just a 'Pretty Posey,' I broke the high school's record for total receiving yards our junior year."

"I had no idea I was the reason behind that impressive achievement," she said, her tone teasing.

She was behind so many things that had been good in his life. Yanking up the collar of his jacket, he said, "I'll grab your suitcase." Tugging the brim of his hat lower over his brow to shield his face from the driving rain, Logan stepped out into the downpour. After grabbing her suitcase from the back of the truck's extended cab, he hurried around to help Hope get down, but by the time he reached her she was already stepping onto the puddled ground below.

Squealing as the cold rain poured down on her, she made a sprint for the front door of the large cedar-sided building, her laughter trailing after her as she left him behind.

Logan followed at a fast jog, suitcase in hand, a grin sliding across his face. He hadn't realized just how much he'd missed hearing Hope's laughter until that moment. "Afraid you're gonna melt?" he asked with a chuckle as he stepped beneath the temporary shelter of the roof's overhang.

She flashed him an impish smile. "Daddy does call me Sugar, you know." Then she turned, hurrying to insert the key into the lock on the door as a gust of wind sent sheets of cold rain past them.

"Stands to reason, then, why you're in such an all-fire hurry to get out of this here downpour," he said. He nearly covered her hand with his own to help steady it, but held back from doing so. He didn't want to remember what it felt like to have her hand in his, something that had once been so natural. As soon as the lock clicked, he reached past her to turn the knob, giving the door a gentle shove open. "Let's get you inside, little darlin'. Can't have you melting into a puddle of sugary sweetness at my feet."

Before he could follow her inside, she turned, her petite form blocking his way. "Thank you for the ride."

"Thank you for the ride?" He looked down at her questioningly. "That sounds like you're sending me off."

"I am," she said, unable to meet his gaze. "There's really no need for you to stick around tonight. All I need to do is close out the register and then I'll head to the house."

His brow tugged upward. "You're asking me to leave you here to walk home in the rain?"

"It's not like it's a long walk," she countered.

She had the right of it. Jack's house sat in a thin copse of pines a few hundred yards behind the main nursery building. "Maybe so," he grumbled, "but I don't like the thought of leaving you here to walk home alone in the dark. In the pouring rain to boot."

"Daddy keeps a handful of umbrellas in his office for customers to borrow on rainy days if they need one."

His concerned refused to budge. At the same time, a tiny voice inside Logan was telling him to back off. That Hope was a big girl. One who was more than capable of making her own decisions in life. Even if they weren't always ones he agreed with. "Reckon I'll be on my way, then. Sleep well," he said with a tip of his hat.

"You, too, Logan." The door closed between them, shutting him out yet again. At least this time it was only a door. Not miles and miles of God's green earth.

Lowering his head, he moved in quickened strides to his truck before he did something foolish like turn around and go back to insist that he escort Hope home. He'd thought he was finally moving past the unrequited feelings he had for her. That time and distance had given him a better grip on his apparently misguided emotions. But he'd been nowhere near prepared for his heart's reaction to spending time with her again. Laughing with her again. Now all he could do was pray.

For Jack to regain his good health. And for himself, knowing there would be no escaping the pain of seeing Hope again, of spending time with her, and knowing her heart would never ever be his.

Chapter Three

"Morning."

Logan's gaze shifted from the plants he'd been watering to find Hope standing in the doorway of the greenhouse. She looked refreshed. More relaxed than she had the day before at the hospital. She wore a sweater beneath an open camel-colored jean jacket. Dark brown leather boots peeped out from beneath the bottoms of her jeans. The long, curling tendrils of her unbound hair looked like a slow-burning fire under the red-gold rays of sunrise.

"Morning," he replied, trying to ignore the sudden thudding of his heart.

"You're here early."

"Habit," he replied as he shut off the hose's nozzle and turned to face her. "Better to start early in my line of work," he explained. "So I'm usually up with the roosters."

"But the nursery doesn't open for business for another couple of hours," she said as she moved past him to walk along two rows of plant-filled tables laden with newly emerging tulips and daffodils. "You could have slept in."

He stood watching her, unable to keep from drinking in the sight of her. "Appears I'm not the only early bird around here."

Reaching out she ran a finger over the droplets of water clinging to a slender green-and-yellow striped leaf of a variegated flax lily. "It appears I had the same idea as you." Letting her hand fall away, she turned to face him. "Watering the plants. Then afterward, before I set out for the hospital, I thought I'd finish tidying up Daddy's office and go through the orders for this coming week."

"You were cleaning his office last night?" After he'd dropped her off more exhausted than not?

"I swept up the broken planter and soil, even repotted the aloe plant with the hope I might be able to save it."

Her words had guilt tugging at his gut. "I'm real sorry you had to do that. I should have at least swept that up before I left for the hospital." Truth was he'd forgotten all about the upturned plant. His focus had been on Jack.

"It's all right," she assured him with a smile.

"I'd rather Daddy have had someone he knew with him at the hospital than concern myself with a little dirt on the floor. Besides, I grew up with a nursery in my front yard. Sweeping up soil spills is one of my many talents."

"Speaking of which, I have bags of topsoil to put out." He set the hose on the floor by his feet. He'd finish watering later, after Hope had gone.

"Why do I get the feeling I'm chasing you away?"

"I have work to do," he grumbled.

"I see," she replied, her scrutinizing gaze fixed upon him.

He sighed. "I'm supposed to be seeing to the nursery during the day so you can spend time with your daddy at the hospital. Or have you changed your mind?" *Like you did with us?*

"Boy, it's starting to sound like a certain someone got up on the wrong side of the bed this morning," Hope teased in the same playful tone she used to use with him when they were teens and he'd had a bad day. It had worked back then. Now it only served to make matters worse.

"With due cause," he replied. "I'm worried about Jack."

"We both are," she agreed. "But there's something else bothering you."

He released a frustrated sigh. "Look, I'm trying to respect your wishes."

Confusion lit her pretty face. "My wishes?"

"That our paths cross as little as possible." And from the way his heart had reacted to the sight of her standing in the greenhouse doorway that morning, respecting her wishes seemed like the smartest plan.

Hope folded her arms in front of her. "I thought we both agreed we were mature enough to put the past behind us while I'm here." Then added, "For Daddy's sake."

She had a point. But then she hadn't been forced to lock away her feelings for him. She didn't have any. So this situation they found themselves in wasn't anywhere near as hard for her as it was for him.

"Judging by that frown on your face, I'm guessing that you're having second thoughts about offering to fill in here while Daddy's down. I'll understand if you wanna withdraw your offer."

Doing so would probably be the wisest thing to do, but he'd made the offer to help out and intended to see it through. "Don't read something into it that's not there. I said I'd lend a hand and I'm gonna do just that."

"Then you don't have a problem with my helping you water the plants?" she asked. While the built-in, overhead sprinkler lines took care of most of the watering in the greenhouses, the various potted plants that lined the inner walls of the glass buildings needed to be hand-watered. "I mean it's not like we've never worked together before."

There had been a time he would have welcomed this opportunity to spend some time alone with Hope. But he was older and wiser, and he wasn't about to let her get under his skin ever again. Because that was what a smart man would do.

Logan motioned to the hose he'd left lying on the ground. "You wanna water? Spray away. Like I told you, I've got other things I can be doing here." Turning, he strode toward the open door.

A few steps away from making his exit, Logan felt the cold, wet spray of water hit him square in the back and travel downward. He froze, unable to believe that Hope had just squirted him with the garden hose. No, soaked him clean through was more like it.

Soft, feminine giggles behind him had him pivoting to face her. Raising an arm to shield his face from the water's relentless spray, he said, "You're playing with fire."

Another giggle. "Then I reckon it's a good thing I've got myself a mighty powerful garden hose to keep that fire from getting out of control."

"Too late," he said with a warning grin as

he charged into the water's cold, wet, arcing stream.

Hope gave a loud shriek as she spun around to flee, dragging the hose behind her.

Three long strides and Logan managed to step on the hose, easily jarring it loose from her grasp. Reeling it in, he took hold of the still-spraying nozzle and aimed it in the direction of Hope's fleeing form. A stream of water went up and over the top of Hope's head, raining down on her. It wasn't a direct hit, one guaranteed to leave her as drenched as he was, but he made certain it was close enough to have her ducking.

"Logan!" she shrieked, arms folded over her head.

This time he was the one chuckling. "You ready to call a truce?" he asked as he shifted the hose's aim to the plants on the table beside her.

"Yes," she sputtered as she turned to face him. Water clung to the spiraling strands of her hair like a heavy morning dew. Coppery curls hung in sagging wet tendrils to frame her face.

A memory came rushing back from the past. One that had been very much like this moment. He and Hope in this very same greenhouse, both armed with hoses. Both soaked clean through by the end of their water play. Both falling in love. Or so he had thought.

I don't love you.

Logan shut off the nozzle's spray and tossed it onto the ground beside him. "You can take it from here. I've got work to do." That said, he walked out of the greenhouse.

Hope stood staring at the empty doorway. What had just happened? Logan's sour mood had turned playful and fun, both of them laughing over the unexpected water battle they'd found themselves engaged in, feeling at ease with each other for the first time in years. Then suddenly he was walking away, his parting demeanor a complete one-eighty from the playful side he'd shown her just moments before.

Pushing the damp curls from her face, she sighed. For the briefest of moments it had felt like old times. Comfortable. Fun. The two of them enjoying life. It had also been a reminder of what she'd given up. Of the forever kind of love she'd come so close to having.

If she were honest with herself, she knew why he'd walked away. And it was fortunate for her that Logan had come to his senses and put an end to things before they got any more carried away. She could never offer him the things he deserved, and the fewer reminders of what they'd once shared the better for them both.

While she'd surprised even herself with her actions, she didn't regret what had happened.

Not completely. Not when their playful respite had helped her to forget about the pain of the past and about the near-paralyzing fear she'd felt before learning that her father was going to be all right.

Hope made her way toward the abandoned hose with a deep sigh. Reaching for it, she turned its nozzle on and began working her way around the inner edges of the greenhouse, watering the vibrantly colored bougainvilleas and other assorted potted plants that lined the glass and metal walls.

Her thoughts turned to her daddy once again. He'd been asleep when she'd called the hospital that morning to check on him. The nurse on duty had assured her that he was still in stable condition, but that his blood pressure was still a little higher than they'd like to see it.

Fear of him having another stroke was always at the back of her mind. She couldn't lose him. For the first time in years, she found herself wanting to pray. Wanting to ask the Lord to help heal her daddy. But praying hadn't brought healing to her mother or to herself. All she could do was hope he was strong enough to get through this health crisis with the help of his very knowledgeable doctors.

When she was through with the watering, Hope gathered up the hose and returned it to the mount near the front wall. Then she stepped out from the protective shade of the greenhouse and into the morning sun. Closing her eyes, she tilted her face upward, welcoming the touch of its warming rays. The air around her smelled of pine and freshly turned soil with a hint of sweetness, no doubt from the flowers blooming inside the greenhouse behind her.

She inhaled deeply, feeling a calm come over her. A feeling of rightness. Because she was back at the nursery. A place that had been like an extension of her own home when she was growing up.

Just like Logan's parents' place had been. Even before she and Logan had begun dating she'd felt like she belonged there, like she was a part of their family. Mostly because their parents had been close friends and had spent a lot of time together at each others' houses. At least they had until her momma had gotten sick and was taken from them. If not for her daddy's love and Logan's momma taking Hope under her comforting wing, she would have been a broken little girl.

If only Logan's momma were here today. Because Hope was feeling very broken now. Like nothing in her life was right. The job she worked. The fast-paced city she had chosen to live in. Her discontented heart. Her abandonment of a faith she had once held so dear. But his momma wasn't here and she was a grown woman who needed to find a way to live with the choices she'd made.

Opening her eyes, she searched the front nursery grounds, hoping Logan hadn't witnessed her moment of self-reflection. Thankfully, he was nowhere to be seen. So she shored up her shoulders and made her way to the storefront, the building that housed the checkout counter, gardening goods for purchase and the office. As she'd told Logan, she needed to look over the calendar and the delivery sheets to see what orders were scheduled to be picked up that week and make certain he would be able to have them ready in time.

Exhaustion mixed with the steady thrum of rain on the office roof had lulled her to sleep in her daddy's big, comfy office chair the night before. When she'd awakened, well into the night, the rain had finally stopped. Too tired to focus, she'd decided to call it a night and made her way back to the house to grab a few more hours' sleep before tackling a new day.

She smiled wistfully as she looked around the main storefront. Her momma had loved this business. She'd built it with Hope's daddy every bit as much as he did. So much so, they'd chosen to name the nursery they opened not long after Hope was born after her.

She moved about the room, tidying each and every shelf. While her daddy had never been one to fret over the fine details when it came to putting up the sale displays, it had been important to her momma. Therefore, it was important to Hope.

Twenty minutes later she stepped back from the assortment of gardening books she had finished sorting alphabetically to glance around the room. She had placed things in a way she felt would present the most appeal to the customers that would be passing through on a daily basis. Everything looked neat and inviting. She had no doubt her momma would have been pleased.

Satisfied, Hope made her way back to the office. Pausing in the doorway, she glanced about the room. The same room she'd nearly lost her daddy in if it hadn't been for Logan. The thought of what might have happened had her stomach turning.

Settling herself into the leather swivel chair, she began sorting through a pile of paperwork. Sales flyers from their suppliers. Paid receipts that needed to be filed away. Purchases that had yet to be billed. Order sheets for pickups. And several letters postmarked as far back as a month ago.

As she was opening those up, she was surprised to find several past due bills from a couple of their suppliers, as well as for some of the utilities. But then in today's day and age her daddy had probably taken care of the payment online and simply hadn't taken the time to mark the paper bills as paid and filed them away. To be sure, she made a mental note to ask him in a day or so, once he got to feeling better.

Gathering up anything she had questions on, she stood and made her way outside to find Logan. This time she spotted him almost immediately, his tall, muscular frame making the trunks of the potted fruit trees look like sticks. He'd pushed his dark, wavy hair away from his face, the still-damp strands glistening beneath the rays of the awakening sun. Logan Cooper was a good man and a hard worker. He always had been. The kind of person who put his heart into everything he did. Just as he was doing now. He could have easily done nothing more than sit back in the office, waiting for customers to require his assistance. But he was seeing to everything her daddy would have taken care of himself were he there to do so.

As she watched him work, she thought back to those few moments they had shared in the greenhouse when no hurt or bitterness, or, as in her case, longing for a life she would never have, hung in the air between them. Only joy and laughter.

Her lips quirked up into a grin as she recalled the stunned expression on his handsome face when she'd taken his advice to "water away."

Logan chose that particular moment to turn her way, his gaze narrowing. "Coming back for round two?" he called out, his husky voice carrying across the yard to where she stood watching him.

"Nope," she said, holding up her empty hands. "No hose. You're safe." It was her heart that wasn't safe. Not around Logan. "I'm sorry I got carried away earlier."

He peered at her past the slender trunks of the young fruit trees that surrounded him. "You didn't look sorry when I caught you watching me with a grin plastered across that pretty face of yours a few moments ago."

That pretty face. How long had it been since she'd heard those words leave Logan's lips? It wasn't the flowery comment that touched her as much as the sweetness in his words where she deserved so much less from him.

"Okay," she conceded. "I'm sorry, but not completely sorry."

One dark brow lifted. "I'm thinking one cancels the other out."

"What I mean is that I regret getting you so

wet," she continued. "But it felt so good to let go and really laugh. I can't recall the last time I did anything like that."

One side of his mouth kicked up into that crooked Cooper grin she so loved. "Reckon I could say the same. Not that I haven't had some fun with my brothers. But what happened back there, well, it felt almost..." His words trailed off, yet she understood.

"Therapeutic?"

"Something like that," he agreed.

"Does that mean I'm forgiven?" she asked and then quickly added, "For getting you wet." To ask for more than that would be asking far too much from him.

"I seem to recall squirting you back," he said as he stepped out from among the potted fruit trees. "So unless you've got hard feelings about my getting even, I'd say there are no apologies needed from either of us."

"I deserved it," she said, her gaze coming to rest on his tan face. "You wanna throw your shirt in Daddy's dryer for a spell? I made fresh coffee this morning. You could help yourself to a cup while you wait."

"Unlike you, darlin', I'm not made of sugar," he replied with a grin. "A little water isn't gonna make me melt. That being the case, I'm fine letting my shirt air-dry."

"Suit yourself," she said with a shrug. *Stubborn man.* "I wanted to talk to you before I left for the hospital. I came across some paperwork that I need to go over with Daddy, but wanted to give you a heads-up on some of the order sheets I found in that stack of paperwork he had lying atop his desk." Holding out her hand, she waited until Logan took the handful of papers from her before continuing, "Two of them are scheduled for pickup the day after next. Another at the end of the week. They were never written down on the calendar."

His gaze came to rest on the orders in his hand and he nodded. "I'll have them ready."

"I can help you get them together when I get home from the hospital tonight."

He looked up. "I think I can handle it on my own."

Meaning he didn't want or need her help. She struggled not to let her hurt show. "Fine. By the way, I finished the watering in the smaller greenhouse. If you could—"

"See to the others," he said, finishing the thought for her just as they'd had a tendency to do for each other back when they were together. "I'll do it as soon as I'm done here."

She nodded, wondering if he even realized what he'd done. How was she supposed to keep the memories at bay when everything about

Logan stirred them up over and over again? "I'll let you get back to work then. I need to go give my hair a quick blow-dry before heading to the hospital. You know how to reach me if you need me." With a nod of acknowledgment from Logan, she walked away, leaving him to his work.

If you need me. Logan watched her go, his emotions all in a tangle. There had been a time when he had needed Hope and yet she'd chosen to walk away. A part of him still wanted her. That part being his heart. His head knew better. Thankfully so.

Hope had made it clear when she'd ended things between them years before that the small-town life wasn't for her. True to her word, she'd settled in a big, busy city, leaving Braxton behind. Leaving those who loved her behind with hardly a glance back.

The times he'd caught sight of her during her infrequent trips home, Hope's discomfort at being there flashed like a beacon on her face. But the smile that had come over her face that morning when they'd had their playful little water battle in the greenhouse had been undeniably real. Her laughter contagious.

It felt so good to let go and really laugh. I can't recall the last time I did anything like that.

Hope's admission had surprised him. The fact that squirting each other with a garden hose had her feeling that way made him wonder if the life Hope had chosen for herself in San Diego hadn't turned out to be all she had wished it would. Not that he needed to concern himself with it. Hope's happiness, or possible unhappiness, was no longer any of his business. Hadn't been for years. Unfortunately for him, old habits die hard and he couldn't seem to stop himself from caring. Not where she was concerned.

The sound of a vehicle rolling up the drive caught Logan's attention. Pulling his cell phone from the front pocket of his jeans, he checked the time. Not quite nine. Hope's Garden didn't officially open for another hour or so.

He stepped from the far right greenhouse and cut through the leafy wall of fruit trees that stood between himself and the parking area, immediately recognizing Ryan's old Chevy truck. The pizza-shaped magnets adhering themselves to the truck's front doors, magnets that advertised his friend's business—Ryan's Pies and Pins—were a dead giveaway. Grinning, Logan peeled off his work gloves and went to greet his friend.

Ryan stepped down, releasing a whistle as his gaze moved over Logan. "You get caught in a downpour the weather station failed to make mention of?"

His thoughts having been distracted elsewhere, he'd forgotten about his still-damp clothes. Giving the clinging flannel shirt a tug, Logan pulled it away from his chest. "I ended up on the wrong end of one of the nursery's garden hoses."

"Jack's still in the hospital, right?"

He nodded.

"Then I reckon I don't have to guess who was holding that hose. Hope always did have good aim."

"Still does," he acknowledged. The three of them had gotten into all sorts of playful water fights during summer breaks in high school. Water balloons, garden hoses, buckets of water, you name it. And Hope usually came out the victor. Mostly because they were soft when it came to her. It was worth losing just to see her smile at besting them.

Ryan shook his head, his grin widening. "Well, she got you good. What'd you do to set her off?"

He shrugged. "Not exactly sure. But I got her back."

Ryan's brow lifted.

"Don't read anything into it," Logan warned. "It wasn't planned."

His friend's grin widened. "Clearly, or you would've brought a change of clothes with you to work today."

"You sticking around for a bit? I've gotta finish watering in the greenhouses before I open up for the day."

"As long as Hope's not waiting in there to douse me."

"You're safe," he assured his friend as they walked back to the buildings. "She's back at the house getting ready to leave for the hospital."

Ryan nodded. "How are you holding up?"

"Better today."

"Glad to hear it. You sounded pretty shaken up last night when you called to let me know what happened."

"For good reason."

"I take it you and Hope have called a truce," Ryan said as he walked beside him.

"It appears that way."

"Reckon it's for the best, seeing as how the two of you are gonna be crossing paths while Jack's in the hospital, not only there but at the nursery, as well. How's Jack doing anyway?" Ryan asked.

"He's holding his own," Logan replied as he pulled open the greenhouse door, motioning Ryan inside. "At least, that's what both of the on-duty nurses told me when I called last night and then again first thing this morning."

"Glad to hear it."

He walked over to the hose that hung in a loose coil from a thick, wooden peg on the wall and began lifting the heavy loops. "I'll look in on him this evening after I lock up here and see for myself. Jack tends to keep things to himself to keep others from worrying."

Ryan's expression grew serious. "If you need anything, help out here, or help with a landscaping job, all you've gotta do is ask."

"I know," Logan said with an appreciative nod. He'd do the same for Ryan. He bent to turn on the spigot and then reached for the nozzle of the hose. "Did you receive the invite?"

"To Nathan and Alyssa's wedding?"

Logan straightened, glancing his friend's way with a sullen expression. "That would be the one. Hearts and flowers and all," he added with a grumble.

Ryan chuckled. "You look as though you just sank your teeth into a lemon. You got something against hearts and flowers?"

"Just not one for weddings," he admitted with a mutter. At least, not any longer. Not since the day he'd gone to see Hope at college with a bouquet of red roses and a box of chocolate-covered pretzels, her favorite, hoping to convince her they were meant to be.

The day she'd ended things once and for all, throwing his declaration of love back in his face by delivering her own declaration that she didn't love him the same way he loved her. So, no, another wedding wasn't something he looked forward to being a part of.

Ryan's expression sobered. "I'm sorry. I don't know what I was thinking. Of course you've got reason to avoid marital festivities. I'm sure Nathan would understand if—"

"No," Logan said, shaking his head. "I'll be there. For Nathan's sake. Just as I was when Carter took a mind to marry Audra. If the good Lord saw fit to bless Nathan with this second chance at true happiness, then I intend to be there for him." He dragged the hose he was holding across the front aisle of the greenhouse and began watering the potted plants that Hope hadn't gotten to.

"Glad to hear it," Ryan said as he followed behind. "The festivities wouldn't be the same without you. Then again, it would leave more wedding cake for me to eat."

"You can have my slice either way," he replied as he moved on to the next plant. "I'm more of a pie man myself."

"I'm gonna hold you to that. So who are you gonna be taking?"

Logan glanced back over his shoulder. "Taking?"

"The 'plus one' that was mentioned on the invitation envelope they sent to us."

He'd completely missed that. He turned back to his watering. "I don't plan on taking anyone. You?"

"Nope," his friend replied. "Weddings tend to give females too many ideas. If a man asks them to accompany them to a wedding as their guest it's a prelude to starting up an actual courtship."

Logan let out a snort of laughter.

"Lizzie will be there," he reminded his friend as he stepped forward, giving the hose a tug behind him.

"Don't start," Ryan grumbled.

He grinned. "When are you gonna open your eyes and realize that Lizzie isn't just your baby sister's best friend? The same one whose ponytail you used to tug on just to rile her when we were growing up."

"Still do," came his friend's muttered admission.

"But for a whole different reason," Logan surmised.

"Don't read anything into it," Ryan said with a grumble, repeating Logan's earlier words.

In Ryan and Lizzie's case he had to wonder if that was true. He reckoned all he could do was sit back and watch to see what path the Lord had chosen for his friend.

As for himself, there was nothing between him and Hope. Never would be again.

Chapter Four

Hope's gaze lifted to the crimson-colored sign that hung over the realty office's entrance. Twin Season Realty was etched into the painted wood plaque in gold lettering. The large picture glass windows on either side of the door were filled with information sheets of homes currently for sale in Braxton and the surrounding areas.

She thought back to the many sleepovers she'd had with her two best friends, Autumn and Summer Myers. All those late-night talks about their plans for their futures. While she would always go on and on about Logan and the family they would someday have together, her friends' plans hadn't included settling down with a family. They had dreamed of starting their own business. Only it was Autumn who had finally seen that dream through to fruition. Summer, the younger twin by just over six minutes, had left Braxton several years before, first for college, and then to "find herself."

Hope had been more than a little surprised to learn of her friend's decision not to return to Braxton. She understood better than most that life didn't always go the way you expected it to.

Her gaze came to rest on the entrance door in front of her as she gathered up the courage to see this through. Nearly losing her daddy had made her realize that there were still so many things left unsaid in her own life. Like the apology she owed both Autumn and Summer for letting the close friendship they'd once shared slip away.

She realized that she hadn't chosen the best way to handle things. Autumn and Summer had been her nearest and dearest friends. They would have been there for her after her diagnosis if she had given them the chance, but at the time it had felt like she was being dragged deep under water and couldn't focus on anything except for fighting her way back to the surface. Leaving Braxton and the life she might have had if things had turned out differently had allowed her to breathe again. But at what cost?

The aroma of hot chocolate drifted past her nose, reminding Hope of the mission she'd come on. The warm drink had been a favorite of their group in high school. She wondered if Autumn would remember. Careful not to spill the insulated cups of the sweet, chocolaty brew that she'd brought with her, she worked the entrance door open and stepped inside.

A quick glance around the lobby revealed that Autumn had been quite successful with her chosen business endeavor. Framed certificates and Realtor awards lined one wall, while pictures of the houses and businesses her friend's realty agency had sold were displayed inside in assorted silver frames on the opposite wall.

Anxiety filled her as Hope called out, "Hello? Anyone here?"

"Be right with you," a familiar voice replied from somewhere in the back. Seconds later stiletto heels clicked atop the dark gray tiled floor as Autumn stepped from her office and headed toward the lobby.

"I heard you were back from Atlanta," Hope said cheerfully the second her friend came into view.

Autumn stopped dead in her tracks, her light blue eyes widening. "Hope?"

"I know you're probably busy," she said, "but I was sort of hoping you might have time to spare for a cup of hot chocolate with an old friend." A part of her waited, expecting Autumn to send her packing.

To her surprise, her childhood friend threw

open her arms and stepped forward to greet her with what promised to be an exuberant hug. "I always have time for an old friend."

Hope took a quick step back, the hot chocolate she'd picked up at Big Dog's on her way to see her friend held securely in her hand. "One sec," she said, laughing as she placed the steaming cups onto a nearby table that held a rack of "homes for sale" magazines. Then she turned and stepped into her friend's welcoming arms.

Autumn squeezed her tight. "It's so good to see you."

"It's good to see you, too."

"When did you get in?" Autumn asked when the hug ended.

"A few days ago," she replied as they stepped apart. "Daddy took ill. He's at County General."

"Oh, no!" her friend gasped. "Is he okay?"

Hope nodded. "He's gonna be." She was determined that it wouldn't be any other way. Her daddy was all she had left in this world.

"Thank the Lord for that."

There was a time she would have done that, but she and the Lord weren't on the best of terms.

"Speaking of which," Autumn continued, "how did you know I was out of town?"

"A little birdie told me." Actually, a very tall,

devastatingly handsome cowboy had, but that was beside the point.

Reaching past Hope, Autumn picked up the plastic-lidded cups and then nodded toward a pair of cushioned armchairs that were flanked by two feathery-fronded parlor palms that sat along the far wall. "Come on in and have a seat."

They crossed the room and settled into the cushy chairs, Autumn handing one of the disposable cups back to her. "It's been so long," her friend said.

A deep sadness filled Hope as she replied, "Since the funeral." They had run into each other at the calling hours for Logan's parents, but their conversation had been brief. Hope had gotten there right before the service began and had to catch a flight back to San Diego right after.

Autumn leaned over to place a comforting hand on Hope's arm. "I know how hard that had to be for you. You were so close to Logan's momma."

"She was like a mother to me."

Her friend nodded. "And you were like a daughter to her."

"I'm so tired of losing the people I love," she said, emotion causing her voice to catch. "Daddy has to get better."

"He will," Autumn said, giving her arm a

comforting pat. "What happened? He seemed in perfect health when I saw him at church last Sunday."

Unlike Hope, her daddy's faith had remained strong despite all the hardships he had suffered. Losing two children due to complications with his wife's pregnancy. Then losing his wife and struggling to keep his business afloat during his time of grief. Even now, when his health had taken a turn for the worse, though only temporarily, he'd held firm to his conviction where God was concerned.

Leaving her own disillusionment with the Lord out of their conversation, Hope went on to tell Autumn what had happened and about her plan to stay in Braxton until her daddy was back on his feet.

"Knowing all that, my next question is how are you holding up?" Autumn asked with a worried expression.

"I'm better now that I've seen how Daddy is doing for myself and have talked to his doctor."

"I wasn't referring to that."

She looked questioningly at her friend.

"I'm talking about your seeing Logan again."

"I saw him at the funeral."

"You know what I mean." Autumn sat back in the chair, taking a sip of her hot chocolate. "It's no secret that you've been avoiding him for years. It's the *why* of it I still haven't figured out."

Hope's gaze dropped to the lid of the insulated cup she held clutched between her hands. "I told you back when I ended things with Logan that our future plans no longer lined up. Coming back to this small town after college didn't have the same lure for me as it did for Logan. I'm where I need to be."

"No change of heart now that you've actually spent some real time with Logan again?"

"If you're asking me if I want things to go back to the way they used to be, then no. I know that's not possible." It was the truth. She hesitated before adding, "So you don't have to worry about me causing any waves between you and Logan."

"Between me and Logan?" Autumn repeated, her slender brows drawn together in confusion.

"You both deserve to be happy." Even if the thought of him dating one of her two closest friends filled her with regret she had no right to be feeling. "He's a good man."

Autumn snorted. "Where in the world did you get the idea that Logan and I are an item? That man is as single as they come."

"He is?" she asked, a misplaced flicker of hope sparking to life inside her. One she needed to douse immediately.

"Oh, he dates on and off. Nothing serious, though, mind you. That man hung up his commitment hat the day you walked out of his life," Autumn explained. "Truth is I think you've ruined him for any other woman. A real waste of a perfect catch if you're into the tall, dark, handsome sort. One who is a kind, caring Christian to boot."

This was the Autumn she remembered. Always speaking honestly. And while she knew her friend would never set out to intentionally cause anyone pain, her words had effectively broken Hope's heart. Knowing that she was to blame for Logan giving up on ever finding love again, Hope's heart pinched painfully.

"That's not how it was supposed to be. Logan was supposed to be married with a bundle of kids by now."

"Kind of hard to do when the woman he loves lives in California," Autumn said, eyeing Hope from over the rim of her cup as she took another sip of the hot chocolate.

"Loved," Hope immediately corrected. "He's finally accepted that there can never be an 'us.'"

Her friend gave another derisive snort. "Says who?"

"Logan," she replied. "He told me so himself."

Surprise lit her friend's tanned face. "I can't believe it."

"Believe it," Hope said, unable to keep the sigh that followed to herself. Thankfully, Autumn didn't seem to notice. If she had, she would have made mention of it. "He didn't want things to become uncomfortable between us during my stay here, since there's no way for us to avoid running into each other and all."

Autumn nodded in understanding. "Logan's pretty close with your daddy. I imagine this has been pretty hard on him, as well."

Hope fingered the lid of her cup, a knot forming at the back of her throat. "If Logan hadn't found Daddy when he did…"

"But he did," Autumn said in a calming tone. "And now that well-timed blessing from the good Lord is gonna give your daddy a second chance at life."

Unlike her momma. Or Logan's parents. And what about Isabel? How could He be considered by so many to be the "good Lord" when there was so much bad that people were left to deal with in their lives?

Autumn set her cup down atop the coffee table and shifted in her chair to face Hope, her expression serious. "Will I see you again since you're gonna be in town a spell? Or should I say my goodbyes now?"

Friends shouldn't have to ask such questions. It should be a given. But then she hadn't been much of a friend to Autumn, or to Summer, for a very long time. Too long.

She missed them. Wanted them back in her life, even if more than a thousand miles separated them. They could call, text, even send letters. Maybe come visit her. The question was, could their friendship be repaired? Would they even want to repair it?

"Autumn," she said regretfully, "I would like very much to get together with you again while I'm here. In fact, letting you know about Daddy wasn't the only reason I stopped by this morning."

"It wasn't?"

"No. I wanted to apologize and hopefully set things right between us again."

"Apologize?" she said questioningly. "For what?"

"For letting our friendship slip away the way I did. I regret it more than you could ever know." There had been no real close female friends in her life since Autumn and Summer, only acquaintances.

"You aren't the only one to blame," Autumn replied, much to Hope's surprise.

"I'm not?"

Autumn sighed. "College took up so much of

my time, between studies and extracurricular activities it was hard for me to focus on anything else. Summer was even busier than I was. So much so, the two of us scarcely saw each other and we were attending the same college. I just figured it was a part of growing up. People's lives heading off in different directions. Even twins had to grow up and become individuals at some point, which Summer and I did. I miss the closeness she and I once shared just as I regret letting our friendship slip away. I could have tried harder to keep in touch with you."

Hope smiled. "I've missed you."

"I've missed you, too," her friend confessed, the faint shimmer of tears pooling in her thickly lashed blue eyes. "Especially after Summer decided to leave Braxton for good."

"I can't imagine how hard it must be for you to have her living in a different town." The two had been inseparable in school, despite the differences in their personalities. Autumn had been a social butterfly. Summer more of an introvert.

"It's not the same," she admitted with a sigh. "But, like you, she's where she needs to be."

Autumn glanced up at the house-shaped clock on the wall and then sat forward in the chair with a gasp. "Oh, no," she said, pushing to her feet. "I almost forgot about a last-minute house showing I scheduled in for this morning. Be right back." Shooting to her feet, she scurried off in the direction of her office, returning a moment later with her jacket on and purse slung over her shoulder. "I'm so sorry to have to rush you off like this."

Hope was already on her feet, half-drunk beverage in hand. "It's all right. I understand. I'm just glad we had a chance to talk."

"So am I," her friend replied with a warm smile as she walked Hope out. "Thank you for the hot chocolate."

"You're welcome."

Opening the beveled glass storefront door, she turned to Hope. "We'll talk again soon?"

"You can count on it." She stepped past her friend and out onto the sidewalk, leaving her to see to her business.

"Tell your daddy I'll be keeping him in my prayers," Autumn called back over her shoulder as she turned to lock the office door behind her.

"I'll do that," Hope replied, her heart feeling so much lighter. "I'm sure he'll appreciate it." With a wave goodbye, she set off down the sidewalk.

To think that she'd nearly backed out of paying her old friend a visit that morning. Thankfully, she'd gone through with it, despite her reservations. Her daddy's health scare had been a stark reminder of how quickly those you cared about could be gone from your life forever. An emotional awakening of sort that had her wanting to start mending fences with those she cared about. Logan included. Even if they could never be anything more than friends.

"There's my baby girl."

Hope returned her daddy's smile with one of her own as she stepped into the private hospital room he'd been moved to for his stay there. "Hi, Daddy." Stepping up to his bed, she bent to kiss his cheek, noting the healthy coloring had finally returned. "How are you feeling today?"

"Restless," he replied.

She laughed softly. "You've only been in here a few days."

"A few too many," he said with a grimace as he eased slightly upright to adjust the flimsy hospital pillow behind him. "How are things at the nursery?"

"Going well," she assured him with a smile as she reached for the visitor's chair, drawing it closer to the bed. *And things would continue to go well*, she thought to herself as she settled onto the seat. She'd make certain of it. Her daddy had never truly asked anything of her, but she would do this for him. Just as he had done so much for her all her life without her ever having to ask.

"And things between you and Logan?"

"Daddy," she groaned. "There is no 'thing'

between Logan and me. We have, however, put the past aside to work together running the nursery until you're able to do so yourself again."

"About that," her daddy said, his expression growing serious.

Hope's heart gave a start. Had her daddy gotten some bad news from the doctor? "Everything's okay," she said. "Isn't it?"

"Other than the fact that my left arm's not ready to cooperate, I'm on the mend. But I've got myself some work to do in physical therapy before I'm back to my old self. I'm hoping to be released real soon."

Her gaze dropped to his weakened arm and then back up to his face. "Do they think you're gonna get full use of your arm back?" she asked, unable to keep the worry from her voice. He'd be lost without the full function of both his arms. Especially in his line of work. Running a nursery could be very physical. A lot of heavy lifting and digging.

He nodded. "With the help of a good therapist and the healing touch of the Lord, I'll be right as rain before you know it."

She released the breath she hadn't even realized she was holding. "I'm so glad. And I can't wait to have you home again. The house isn't the same without you."

He smiled. "That's nice to know. I thank the

Lord that I've had you and Logan to take care of things at the nursery for me while I've been laid up in this place."

"Speaking of which—" she began reaching into her oversize leather purse for the paperwork she'd brought with her "—I came across some things when I was cleaning off your desk that I want to go over with you if you're up to it?"

"Things?"

"Nothing major. A few order sheets. A couple of bills that, if you haven't already paid them online, are past due."

His brows creased. "Past due?" He held out a hand. "Let me have a look."

She handed the assorted papers over to him.

Her daddy sifted through them, a frustration pulling at his mouth. "I remember getting these in," he said, studying the bills. Then his graying brows furrowed as his gaze shifted back to her. "Only I can't recall whether or not I ever paid them."

"I couldn't find anything that said you had," she told him. "Would you have paid them online? Because the envelopes hadn't even been opened. They were just mixed in with a bunch of other miscellaneous papers."

A nurse stepped into the room, temporarily interrupting their conversation. "How are we doing today, Mr. Dillan?"

"I'd be a lot better if you'd let me go home," he muttered. "But while you're in here, got anything in that medicine basket of yours to help an old man's memory?"

She placed a tiny plastic cup filled with pills onto the table beside the hospital bed. "Your leaving is up to the doctor, but I don't think they'll be keeping you in here a whole lot longer. The newest dosage of medication seems to be getting your blood pressure down to where we like to see it." She reached for the water pitcher and filled his empty cup halfway. "As for something to jar your memory, you should see some improvement with that now that your blood pressure is leveling out. High blood pressure can cause all sorts of medical issues, confusion and forgetfulness being among them."

"I had no idea," he said, his frown etching even deeper into his tanned face.

"It's okay, Daddy," Hope said, not wanting him to get upset over something that would be straightened out with some medication adjustment and a little time. "All that matters is you're getting well enough to come home soon."

"Your daughter's right," the nurse agreed. "You need to focus on getting well. I'm gonna be going off duty in about twenty minutes. Is there anything else I can get you before I leave?"

He shook his head.

"Okay, I'll see you tomorrow."

"Daddy?" Hope asked when the nurse had gone. "Is there something else troubling you?"

He looked up at her. "It's about the nursery."

She reached for his hand, covering it with her own. "The nurse and I told you not to worry about that right now."

"I have to, honey," he said, giving her hand a loving squeeze. "There's something I've been meaning to run past you."

He sounded so serious. "If this is about my staying in town longer, I promise that's not even an issue. I told you I have time built up that I can use to extend my stay here if necessary."

"Sugar," he said, meeting her gaze, "I'm not asking for you to stick around for days or weeks. What I'm asking is for you to come home for good and take over the running of Hope's Garden."

She blinked hard—twice—certain she'd heard him wrong. "Daddy, do they have you on some sort of pain medication?"

He chuckled. "Not a lick. My head's as clear as that big blue Texas sky outside."

She would love nothing more than to come home for good. But being back in Braxton, so near to the man she could never have, but who would forever hold her heart, left her far too vulnerable to feelings she'd spent years trying to forget.

She shook her head. "I can't just quit my job and move home. I have a career. And there's the lease I signed on my apartment."

"I figured that might be the case," her daddy said, sounding disappointed all the same. "But I wanted to make the offer to you before I consider other options."

"Other options?"

"If you weren't interested in coming back and taking over the family business, I thought I might offer Logan an equal partnership if he agreed to run the nursery. Maybe even give him the option of buying me out in the next year or so."

She gasped. How could he even consider doing something like this? He loved the business he had built. "Why would you do that?"

"Because that boy knows what he's doing," her daddy replied matter-of-factly. "And I've done a fair amount of thinking since I've been lying here in this here hard-as-a-rock hospital bed with nothing to do but twiddle my thumbs. The Lord Almighty gave me a wake-up call this week, reminding me that I'm not getting any younger. It's high time I reprioritize my life."

"You're not old," she argued, refusing to hear

him talk that way. "Not old enough to think about retiring."

"Darlin', I've spent most of my adult years running that place," he reminded her with a tender smile. "After your momma died, it gave me an outlet to take my mind off my grief. At least for the hours I spent working. And when you moved away, Hope's Garden became my life. But there's more to a person's existence than working day in and day out. I'm ready to do some traveling while I'm still healthy enough to enjoy it. Maybe even buy myself a fifth-wheel and do some camping."

Had the stroke affected Daddy's mind? Because this was not the man she knew. Her daddy didn't just run off to go camping. He stuck around and tended to his responsibilities. Hope's Garden being at the top of that list.

"Please hold off on asking Logan until you've had a chance to really think this out. A decision like the one you're considering needs to be made with a clear head, and only after a great deal of consideration."

"Sugar, time isn't on my side right now. I've got to be realistic. My recovery could take a while and I've worked too hard to let Hope's Garden go belly-up when I have options. And from the look of things," he said, his gaze dropping to the papers he held in his hand, "it's on its way, leaving bills unpaid the way I did."

"That wasn't your fault," she said in his defense.

"It might not have been intentionally," he said, "but what if I start having blood pressure issues again? Or another stroke? I need to have things lined up to protect the business I built to assure that you're taken care of in case the good Lord decides to call me home."

"He's not calling you anywhere," she blurted out, her eyes tearing up. She couldn't even bear to hear him talk about the possibility.

His smile softened. "Not yet, sugar. But the day will come, God willing many, many years down the road, and I want to have my life in order when it does."

She resisted the childish urge to cover her ears, wanting to block out his words. She hadn't come here to discuss his dying. She needed her daddy to dive back into life, to return to his passion for gardening and growing the best selection of perennials and annuals in the entire county, maybe even the whole state of Texas.

"Daddy," she said, trying to keep her emotions in check, "Logan already has a full-time business of his own to run. He can't very well take on another."

"He's in the landscaping business," her daddy

said as if she'd forgotten that fact. Not that she'd ever forget anything that had to do with Logan Cooper. "Owning a nursery would be a plus for him," he continued determinedly. "He'd get all of his plants and trees for his landscaping jobs at rock-bottom prices. No more haggling with me over cost."

She gasped at Logan's audacity. "He haggled with you over your prices?" Maybe she didn't know Logan as well as she thought she did. Her daddy had the fairest prices around on his plants and trees. "How dare he try to get you to come down even more!"

"Hope, honey," her daddy said, trying to calm her, but she wasn't having it.

"I mean it, Daddy. Just let him try to get those prices anywhere else in the county!" So much for keeping her emotions in check.

Her daddy's face split into a grin. "It's good to see that San Diego hasn't taken all of that inner fire out of you. But you can lower the flame in this case, darlin'. Logan doesn't try to haggle me *down* on my prices. That boy is always trying to haggle me *up*."

For the second time since entering her daddy's hospital room, Hope blinked in surprise. "Up? As in he wanted to pay you more than you were asking?" Even as she asked the question, she knew that would be something the Logan she had known would do. He was generous to a fault. And she had no doubt his offering to pay more for items purchased from the nursery was meant to help her daddy out financially. Not that he'd needed to do that. He wasn't rich, but her daddy was able to live more than comfortably.

"He's a good man," her daddy said, carefully watching her response to his words.

She couldn't deny it. Hope gave a slow nod and said with a sigh, "He is. I'm glad you have him here to look out for you." Since his own daughter couldn't be there to do so, she thought to herself, guilt weaving its way through her.

"I'd like to have you here fussing after me, too," he said, looking up at her in silent pleading.

"Daddy..."

"Sugar, I know you think the big city is where you wanna be, but I also know you and you're not happy there. Not as happy as you should be," he stated. "I hear it in your voice every time you call. See it in your eyes every time you come home. The longing for all those things you left behind. Logan included."

Had she done that poorly at hiding her feelings? "What you heard was me missing you," she told him. "And, of course, I miss Braxton. I spent most of my life here."

"And Logan?" he pressed.

She turned away and stepped over to the window to peer out through the open slats of the glass-encased miniblinds. "I miss what we had," she admitted with a soft sigh. "But you and I both know that life doesn't always go the way we plan for it to go."

"Logan Cooper," a female voice chirped behind him. "Don't tell me you got yourself booted out of that there hospital room already?"

Logan turned from where he stood just outside the entrance to Jack's room to see Verna Simms standing there, friendly smile on her face, carryout bag from her diner dangling from the crook of her arm.

Inside the room, all talk ceased.

He wanted to groan at the position he'd been caught in. He hadn't been eavesdropping. Not intentionally. He'd simply had the bad timing of showing up right when Hope and her daddy were discussing him. Joining them in the room would have been uncomfortable for all, so he'd opted to wait until the conversation moved on to something that didn't involve him. Now it was too late.

He straightened, clearing his throat. "No, ma'am. I just got here myself," he said a little louder than necessary. But the last thing he wanted was for Hope to think he was invading her privacy. Or, even worse, being a snoop.

The older woman's smile lifted even higher. "Jack is a blessed man to have so many people who care about him. Speaking of caring, I was just popping in to bring him some of my home-made chicken noodle soup." She leaned forward to add, "Light on the salt." That said, she swept past him into the room.

Having no choice now that his presence had been made known, Logan followed her in. Hope's reply to her daddy echoed in his thoughts as he prepared to face her. *I miss what we had.*

"Hope," Verna greeted with a warm smile.

"Verna," Hope replied as the older woman moved toward Jack's bed.

"Well, well," she said with a playful click of her tongue, "seems to me you'll do just about anything for some of my cooking."

"Darlin', I'd much rather be eating your cooking at the diner than lying here in this here hospital bed being a human pincushion," Jack replied with a wide grin as he looked up at Verna.

Her laughter filled the room. "Stop being such a baby. The nurses are just doing their jobs."

The conversation between Jack and Verna, light and playful, went on, but Logan's attention strayed to Hope, who was standing by the window on the far side of the bed. Her refusal to look at him confirmed what she thought he'd been doing.

With a sigh, he crossed the room to stand beside her, his gaze moving to Jack who, at that moment, was smiling up a storm. "How's he doing?"

"Aren't you supposed to be watching the nursery?" Hope muttered, still avoiding his gaze. A tinge of pink had spread across her pretty face. Anger or embarrassment, he wasn't quite sure.

"Nathan's holding down the fort for me until I get back," he explained. "I have a few new orders I needed to go over with your daddy." He held up the manila folder he'd brought with him from the nursery.

"He's in the hospital," she said in whispered warning. Then her green eyes lifted. Yep, she was mad. There was no denying the sparks he saw filling those big, beautiful eyes of hers. "Couldn't you have handled the orders without having to involve him?"

Logan could hear loud and clear what she really meant by her words. *Couldn't you have handled them without coming here where I might be forced to spend even more time with you than I'm already being subjected to?* Then he recalled her words to Jack just moments before. *I miss what we had.* Maybe her anger when he'd stepped into the room stemmed more from the embarrassment of him having overheard her admission than from her thinking he had done so on purpose.

He shouldn't care that a part of Hope still longed for what they'd once shared, but he did. To a man who had spent years trying to stay afloat in a never-ending sea of what-ifs, her words were like having a piece of hope float by.

One he knew he should let pass him by. But Lord help him, he couldn't. Not completely. She'd hurt him. He'd never be able to trust her fully again. Yet, the Lord had brought her back into his life for a reason. Maybe to finally put things to rest between them. All Logan could do was hold faith in the Lord to lead him in the direction he was meant to go.

He looked down into Hope's big, beautiful, if not a little angry, green eyes and said, keeping his voice low, "If I were the owner of Hope's Garden, yes. As it stands, I'm not. Therefore, Jack needs to give his approval on the quotes I've done up on any of the larger orders that come in."

He resisted the urge to tell her how pretty she looked, despite the irritated glare she was sending his way. Jack was who he had come there to see. He couldn't allow himself to be sidetracked by Hope or what feelings might still linger there between them. Not when there was work to do back at the nursery. Turning away, he stepped over to the bed.

Verna glanced up when Logan joined them, a bright smile still lighting her face. "I should be getting back to the diner and give you three a chance to visit."

"But you just got here," Jack said in as close to a whine as Logan had ever heard.

Logan muffled a chuckle.

"Wyatt could only come in and cover for me for a couple of hours today, so I need to get back. Not all of us get to lounge around in bed and be pampered by nurses all day," she told him with a teasing grin as she zipped up her spring jacket.

Logan did chuckle aloud this time.

"Pampered?" Jack repeated with a derisive snort. "That's what you call getting ordered around, stuck with needles and losing a good night's sleep to get my blood pressure and temperature taken practically every hour on the hour?" He gave another snort for good measure.

Verna leaned forward, giving him a gentle pat on the cheek. "You poor dear. Best get better soon, then." Straightening, she looked up at Logan. "I'd appreciate it if you'd keep me updated on this stubborn mule's progress."

He nodded. "I'll be sure to."

"Tell your nephew thank you," Jack grumbled.

Verna looked his way. "For what?"

"For covering for you at the diner so you could come pay me a visit and bring me some of your homemade chicken noodle soup."

"I'll do that," she replied, a smile softening the corners of her mouth. She swung her attention back to Logan as she picked up her purse from the chair by the hospital bed. "Be sure to tell Hope to give me a call if she needs anything."

Tell Hope? Couldn't Verna just tell her that herself? Before Logan could respond, Verna was gone. He glanced back over his shoulder to find that Hope had slipped away, as well.

Chapter Five

"Give her time," Jack said, drawing Logan's gaze his way. "She'll come around."

"Time isn't gonna change anything," he replied. "You'll be up and about soon and Hope will be back in California living her life."

"Not as soon as I'd like," Jack said with a sigh. Then, catching himself, added, "Not the Hope leaving part, mind you, but the getting back on my feet part." He attempted to lift his weakened arm. "This here uncooperative arm of mine is gonna take some coaxing to get it back to where it needs to be."

"Then you'll coax it," Logan said. Whatever it took to get his friend back to his old self.

"You can count on it, son," the older man said determinedly. "The good news is the doc is hopeful that I'll get back full or near to full use of it."

"And the bad news?"

"Is that it could take up to twelve weeks for that to happen. Hope and I were just discussing this before you and Verna arrived."

Among other things, Logan thought, recalling the part of their conversation he'd chanced upon when he'd gotten there.

Twelve weeks? That was a long time to be physically limited in Jack's line of work. "What about the nursery?" he asked in concern. He'd be able to help out some, but he had contracted jobs coming up that would take up a good bit of his time. How was Jack going to handle things on his own when he was physically incapacitated?

"Something I've been mulling over," he said as he lifted the sheet that covered him and shoved it aside. Then he sat up, swinging his legs over the edge of the bed as he pushed to his feet.

"Should you be getting up without a nurse?" Logan asked worriedly.

"I'm not an invalid." He made his way over to the window where he stood peering out at the wooded area that lined the rear grounds of the hospital. "But yes, I'm allowed. In fact, they want me to stretch my legs some, but I'm to do so 'slowly.'" He glanced back at Logan, his expression one of frustration. "Do I look like a tortoise to you?"

Unable to help himself, Logan grinned.

"Never mind," Jack grumbled, his gaze returning to the bright, sunlit day outside. "Getting back to what we were discussing, I've done some mulling over things these past few days and have made some decisions that involve both you and my daughter."

"What kind of decisions?"

His friend turned from the window. "You have time to take a walk down to the waiting area while we talk?"

Logan nodded. "Nathan's watching over the nursery while I'm here." Remembering his own reason for being there, he held up the folder of order sheet quotes he'd put together for some of the larger orders that had come during Jack's absence. "When you feel up to it, you can look these over and give me final approval before I get back to your customers."

"No need," Jack said, waving the folder away. "I trust you to handle things at the nursery while I'm away. Everything."

"That means a lot."

Jack struggled to pull on his robe with his weak arm.

Logan stepped forward to give him a hand.

The older man mumbled his appreciation, no doubt finding it hard to deal with needing others to do for him what he'd always been able to do on his own, then started for the open door.

"My trust in you is a big part of the reason I need to have a few words."

"If this has something to do with Hope and my relationship," Logan said, following Jack out of the room, "I don't want you expecting more than what it is."

"While I admit to wishing there could have been more between the two of you, this has to do with the nursery," he explained as they walked side by side down the long, dimly lit corridor. "I had a long talk with Hope earlier. I've asked her to consider coming home and taking over the business."

Logan nearly missed a step. Jack and Hope had done a lot of serious talking that day. "She's moving back to Braxton?"

Jack shook his head. "If I said yes, that would be putting the cart before the horse. I asked my daughter to consider it. She hasn't agreed. Not yet anyway. In fact, she gave me all the reasons why she couldn't."

"I take it I was one of them," Logan muttered knowingly.

"Actually, no," Jack said, much to Logan's surprise. "Her job. Her lease. All things she can work around if she truly has a mind to."

"So you think there's a chance she might change her mind about coming home to run the nursery?" Did he have to sound so hopeful?

Logan wanted to give his own self a firm kick for reacting the way he had.

"She hasn't given me a definite no. So I'm still holding out some hope that she'll have a change of heart," Jack admitted as they ambled at a slow pace down the hallway. "But you and I both know there are no guarantees in life."

Logan nodded in agreement. Did he ever.

"Therefore," his friend continued, "I'm gonna go ahead and start making those changes in my life I've come to realize need to be made. That being the case, I'd like to make you an offer."

Logan glanced his way. "An offer?"

"I'd like you to come in as a partner at the nursery," Jack explained. "With the possibility of buying me out completely if Hope decides not to take on my half of the business by the time I'm ready to step away from it fully. I'd like to keep it at least partially in the family, but I'll respect whatever decision she makes."

"That's all you can do," Logan agreed, just as he'd had to accept Hope's decision that things would never work out between them.

They reached the waiting area and Jack motioned for Logan to take a seat as he settled himself into one of the other vinyl-covered chairs. "This is where you come in. I have come to think of you as the son I never had, so in my heart I would still be keeping Hope's Garden in the family if I brought you into the business."

Logan was floored by the unexpected offer, as well as touched by Jack's heartfelt words. But he wasn't at a place financially where he was ready to invest into another business. Besides, Hope's Garden was Jack's baby. How could he even consider parting with it? If even only partially.

"Maybe you should take some more time to think this out," Logan suggested. "Some medications impair a person's ability to make reasonable decisions, operate large machinery and whatnot."

Jack chuckled. "You sound just like my daughter when I brought this up with her. But like I told her, I'm as clearheaded as they come."

"Jack, I'm honored that you would consider bringing me in as a partner. But to be honest, I'm not sure I'd be able to come up with the cash needed to do that right now. Then there's trying to find time to run both Cooper Landscaping and Hope's Garden."

"That's what employees are for. We can hire someone to help out at the nursery after Hope has to return to her job in California. Whatever it takes, son, I'm willing to work something out," Jack said determinedly.

He knew the amount of trust Jack was placing in him to make such an offer. If they could hire on one or two people to run the nursery, then that would free him up to continue doing landscaping jobs. Although he might have to cut his workload back some to ensure he'd be able to put some time in at the nursery. But he had no doubt he could be a worthy business partner for Jack. He already knew how to run his own. And he knew enough about the various plants and trees Hope's Garden sold and what care each and every one of them required.

Logan let out a long sigh. "I need to be honest with you, Jack."

"I'd expect no less from you, son."

"As honored as I am, as tempted as I am to consider your offer, I wouldn't want Hope thinking that I'm trying to take advantage of her daddy when he's down."

"I think she knows you better than that," Jack replied.

Problem was Logan didn't know her. Not any longer. Maybe he never really knew Hope, because to this very day nothing made sense to him about their breakup.

They'd been happy and while they may have had differences of opinion on some things, they'd never let it cause issues between them. They'd shared dreams and attended church together. They'd talked about the kids they would someday have. Even going so far as to choose the names they wanted for their future children.

Then right before high school graduation everything changed. Hope stopped wanting to talk about their future together. She smiled less. Attended church less. She put the blame on her need to focus on college. To find herself.

He fought the urge to frown at the memory. How could he have felt closer to Hope than anyone else ever in his life, his brothers included, and not know she was feeling lost? Had leaving helped her to finally find herself? Or was she still searching for that part of her that was missing?

"You still love my baby girl." It wasn't a question.

"Fool that I am," Logan admitted with a sigh.

"You're not a fool," Jack said firmly. "You're a man who loves deeply. And my gut tells me my daughter still has feelings for you, as well. I know you and I have talked about what happened. Maybe not so much in the recent years, but I still can't seem to make sense of it."

"Well, seems we're both still in the same boat," Logan muttered. "Probably won't ever know."

"Reckon we have to keep in mind that love is patient. Maybe someday we'll have the answers we're searching for."

He'd heard that phrase mentioned during the

exchange of wedding vows between his brother and Audra. But as far as he was concerned, he'd been more than patient when it came to Hope.

"At the very least, find it in yourself to forgive her," Jack suggested. "The heart can't heal the way it should when there's anger festering there."

Could he truly forgive Hope for what she'd done? And what if it had been something he'd done or said, that had caused her feelings toward him to change? Anything was possible, he reckoned.

All he knew was that his head was telling him to guard his heart around Hope, without a doubt the safer route for him to take. But his heart had never been one to listen to reason. If it did, Logan would have stopped loving her a very long time ago.

Chapter Six

Logan stepped from the greenhouse that housed the flowers, carrying a large tray of annual flats he would use to replace the ones customers had purchased over the past few days.

Jack had built himself up a good solid business. One he'd offered Logan a piece of if he wanted it. Did he want it? There were so many good memories for him there at the nursery. Like the very first day he started working for Jack. He had just turned sixteen and was ready to prove himself every bit as capable of earning his own money as his two older brothers.

But he'd earned more than money the two years he'd spent working at Hope's Garden. He'd earned Jack's respect and his trust where dating Hope was concerned. Not an easy feat, considering how protective his friend was of his daughter.

Jack had packed away all of his grief for the wife he'd lost and had devoted his life to raising and nurturing his only child. Hope had been working alongside her daddy at the nursery for years, learning the family business. So when Logan was hired on there, he and Hope got to know each other even better, and, like the flowers they tended to, their relationship blossomed and grew into something more.

His thoughts went to the day Hope had ended things between them to go off and find herself in the world, leaving his heart, which held no use for him any longer, to wither and wilt. Not that he'd allowed anyone to know just how deeply her leaving had hurt him. Instead, he spent his days laughing and playing jokes, while inside he felt as scattered and broken as the town had been after the tornado.

Until now.

Something about her return, the way Hope looked at him when she thought he wasn't looking, hearing that she missed what they'd had together, had him thinking what if…

What if he completely forgave her? Set his anger aside? If he put himself out there, put his heart on the line once again, would the past repeat itself? What if he didn't and he spent the rest of his life wondering if things might have been different this time around?

"Uncle Logan!" His niece's voice filled the greenhouse, bringing an instant smile to his face.

Setting the flat of ornamental cabbage down onto the table, he turned to face her, his smile widening. "Well, if it isn't our little Katydid," he said, using the playful nickname he and his brother Carter had given their oldest brother's little girl. He bent to catch her up in his arms. He and Carter adored their niece and had helped Nathan with the raising of her after Isabel's untimely passing.

"I get to buy some flowers to plant by our porch," she announced excitedly as he carried her out of the domed greenhouse and into the sunshine.

"Got plenty of those here," he told her as he lowered her back down onto her feet. He looked around, searching for his brother. Nathan's pickup was parked under the shade of a distant tree, but his big brother was nowhere to be seen. His gaze dropped down to his niece. "You drive here on your own?"

She giggled. "No, silly. You have to be a big person to drive a truck. And wear a cowboy hat," she added with a smile that displayed a small gap where two of her bottom baby teeth used to be and two new ones were pushing up to fill the space.

Logan reached out to ruffle Katie's dark curls. "Where'd your daddy get off to?"

"He's home painting the back porch. It was Miss McCall's idea to come here. She's still in the truck 'cause she had to answer a work call."

His gaze snapped back in the direction of the pickup. "Alyssa drove you here?" What could she have been thinking? With her visual impairment, she had risked both of their lives as well as anyone they might have passed along the way.

Soft, feminine laughter sounded behind him. "Hardly."

He turned to see Audra, Carter's wife, walking up to join them.

"Alyssa makes a much better copilot. Afternoon, Logan," his sister-in-law greeted with a smile. "I was taking a look at Jack's selection of shade trees. Carter's going to plant a couple in the front yard for me. I'm supposed to pick out the ones I want and then he'll stop by to pick them up once they're finished digging."

"They?"

"Carter has enlisted the assistance of our children," she explained. "Actually, they volunteered their services with such enthusiasm your brother couldn't bring himself to refuse. So I left them to do the digging while I picked up Alyssa and Katie, who offered to accompany me here."

Our children. Oh, how he longed for a family like both of his brothers had. However, the Lord appeared to have other plans for him. Like being the best uncle in the entire world. Which he had to admit he succeeded in doing quite well. "See anything you like?"

"Several," she replied with a nod. "Looks like I might have to help dig the additional holes. But it'll be worth it. I so love a large front yard with shade trees in it."

His gaze dropped to her rounded belly. Audra was due to have her baby around the end of May, but he had his doubts the baby boy she was carrying was going to wait that long. "Dig holes in your condition? I can pretty much guarantee Carter's not gonna allow that to happen."

She glanced down, her sweet smile softening all the more. "You're probably right."

"Tell you what," he said. "You pick out the trees you want and as soon as I close up here for the day I'll load them up and bring them out to your place. Seeing as how your favorite brother-in-law is a landscaping specialist, I'll have them in the ground before you can say 'Dinner's ready.' Deal?"

Her bright smile widened. "Logan Cooper, are you inviting yourself to dinner?"

"Reckon that would be the case. Come on, Audra, take pity on this poor, wifeless bachelor?" he pleaded playfully.

"Maybe you can find a wife at the toy store," Katie piped up excitedly. "That's where Daddy found Miss McCall."

Logan gave a husky laugh. It was true that Nathan had first crossed paths with Alyssa at The Toy Box, the town's long-standing toy store. Actually, it had been in front of the store. However, contrary to his adorable little niece's misconception, the toy store did not stock a ready supply of wives for men who were shopping for one of their own. Something he was not in the market for anyway. "Thank you for the wife-hunting advice, Katydid," he said with a grin. "I'll be sure to keep that in mind."

She seemed pleased with his reply. "And don't forget the mistletoe. That's what makes two people fall in love and get married."

A little out of season for mistletoe, but he nodded all the same. "Duly noted."

"Sorry to hold things up," Alyssa said as she hurried over to where they stood talking. "Flooring issues. The supplier sent mahogany planks. Nathan's client ordered oak."

His soon-to-be sister-in-law had been staying at The Cat's Cradle after moving permanently to Braxton following her engagement to

Nathan. The local boardinghouse was owned by two very kind, very eccentric elderly sisters, who had taken Alyssa under their wing when she'd first come to town to help with the rec center. And then his oldest brother, in a very wise business move, hired her on to handle the interior design for any of the jobs his and Carter's construction company contracted that required her line of expertise. While Alyssa had been left visually impaired as the result of a car accident, she hadn't lost her God-given talent for interior design.

"I can see how that could be an issue," Logan said with a nod. "But you weren't holding us up." He glanced down at his niece. "Katie here was advising me on how to find myself a wife."

"She was? Hmm…I didn't realize you were in the market for one," Alyssa teased, knowing that marriage was no longer even an ink spot on the to-do list for his life.

"You mean he can find a wife in the grocery store, too?" Katie asked in awe, her dark brown eyes wide.

Audra smothered a giggle. "I'm sure it's been done before. Or your uncle Logan could drive around town, looking for women who have gotten themselves stuck on rickety old porch roofs."

Katie nodded in agreement, having heard the story of how her uncle Carter had rescued her aunt Audra from her porch roof, after which they fell in love and got married.

The conversation, while entertaining, was getting too far off track for Logan's comfort. Especially with the direction some of his thoughts had taken since Hope's return. Before his niece had the chance to respond to Audra's playful comments, he asked his sister-in-law, "You said you found some trees you liked?"

"About a dozen," she answered, grinning.

"A dozen?" Alyssa gasped. "Can we fit that many in the back of the truck?"

"We won't have to," Audra replied. "I'm going to limit myself to six. I wouldn't want Logan to miss out on the dinner I'm going to make for him tonight, because he's still outside planting my trees. Which, I might add, he has so graciously offered to do so I won't have to."

"I bribed her," he admitted with a chuckle. "Dinner in exchange for my expert and expedient planting services."

"Can't blame you," Alyssa said. "I'd use whatever means necessary myself to be fed her cooking." She looked to her future sister-in-law. "Audra's cooking is right up there with Verna Simms." A compliment if ever there was one.

"And she makes really good pies," Katie blurted out.

"All these compliments," Audra said, blushing slightly. "Tell you what. How about we do a family dinner tonight? How does lasagna with salad and garlic bread sound?"

"And pie?" Katie said, her dark eyes looking up at Audra pleadingly.

"And pie," she agreed, smiling down at her niece.

"You don't have to do that," Alyssa said. "It's not even Sunday."

Sunday suppers were family time, getting together at either Nathan's or Carter and Audra's place to eat, visit and then, if time allowed, participate in some Bible study together.

"I want to," Audra replied, her gaze shifting to Logan. "I'd like for you to invite Hope to join us."

Surprise lit his face at her request. Then his mouth tugged downward. "Katie, honey, why don't you head back into the greenhouse and start choosing your flowers? We'll join you in a moment."

"Okay," his niece chirped, oblivious to the sudden unease that filled him with Audra's request.

"Watch you don't trip on the garden hose I've got laying on the floor," he called after her as she skipped away, her limp, a permanent reminder of the tornado that hit Braxton a little over two years before, now barely noticeable.

Once she had gone, he turned back to his sister-in-law. "I don't think inviting Hope to join us for dinner would be a very good idea."

"Surely the two of you can get along through one dinner," she said emphatically.

"It isn't that." He and Hope had managed to remain amicable since her return, their focus centered on Jack's needs instead of their own. "I'm not so sure Carter or Nathan would appreciate having her join us. They didn't take too kindly to her shutting me out the way she has." He hadn't, either, but his was more hurt than anger. But then they were his big brothers. It was only natural for them to feel the need to have his back.

"You leave Carter's mind-set to me," Audra told him. "Besides, Jack is a close friend of the family. You wouldn't want him worrying over his daughter's well-being when he should be spending his energy on getting better himself."

"I agree," Alyssa said. "I know there's some past hurt between the two of you, but maybe it's time to put it behind you."

"Which means forgiving her," Audra nodded.

He knew they meant well, but complete forgiveness tended to be harder to give when human emotions were involved. But he was trying. He needed to forgive Hope and finally move on with his life. That meant getting his heart to accept what couldn't be changed. If only he could push the conversation he'd overheard between Hope and Jack from his mind.

"It can't be easy for Hope," Audra went on, drawing Logan from his thoughts.

He glanced at his sister-in-law. "She's the one who ended things."

Audra reached out, placing a gentle hand on his forearm. "I was referring to her only remaining parent being in the hospital with a serious health scare. We know how hard it is to lose both of our parents. Jack's close call had to have shaken Hope badly."

Alyssa nodded. "Add that to her having to remain for who knows how long in a place that holds so many memories for her, both good and bad. She's pretty much being forced to mend fences she might not have been emotionally ready to mend yet."

I'm that fence, Logan thought with a deepening frown. How could nine years not be long enough to be emotionally ready? Unless…

I miss what we had.

Hope's words were stuck like a burr to his thoughts. Once again, he had to ask himself if it was possible she had put so much effort into avoiding him because deep down she still cared? Was she afraid he would reject her as she had him years before?

In that moment Logan made his decision. He

would forgive. But he was also going to find out the truth of it. It was a risk, but one he felt the need to take. He just prayed the Lord would give him the strength to pick up the pieces of his heart if Hope chose to cut him out of her life all over again.

"We'll be there," he told Audra. Now he just had to find a way to convince Hope to join him.

Hope was emotionally drained by the time she left the hospital. She'd been fielding work calls on and off for most of the day. Apparently, taking personal time off didn't constitute a complete reprieve from the demands of her job, handling marketing for Complete Solar Management. She had to admit that it helped to keep her thoughts from straying to Logan Cooper and that charming, slightly crooked grin of his.

And then there was her worry over her daddy's slower than expected recovery. His left arm was still weak and his blood pressure still a little higher than they would like it to be, which meant he couldn't be released to come home just yet.

Home. Where she needed him to be. Where she needed to be. Tears spilled onto her cheeks, sliding downward in warm, moist trails.

She hadn't realized how much she'd missed

being there until this past week. Her previous trips home had been short and had consisted of spending time at the nursery.

She'd avoided running into people from her past, knowing they would inevitably ask how she was doing. Putting on a smile and telling people she was happy with her life was hard to do.

With a soft sniffle, she turned onto the drive leading to Hope's Garden. Her traitorous gaze immediately began searching for Logan. Just as it had done every day for the past four days Logan had been covering for her at the nursery.

She didn't want to feel this overwhelming need to see him at the end of the day, but it was there all the same. Despite their past, or maybe because of it, Logan had become a strong shoulder to lean on, an ear to share her concerns with, a friend in the life of solitude she'd built around herself, both here and in San Diego.

It was the ease with which she and Logan had fallen into an amicable relationship that scared her senseless. It would be far too easy to forget her reasons for pushing Logan away. Too easy to want to be a part of his life again. But that wouldn't be fair to him. And for that reason alone, she could never let the emotional wall that she'd put up between them down completely. No matter how badly her heart ached to let him back in.

She really needed to pull herself together before she walked down to the nursery to relieve Logan and close out that day's sales. The telltale water glistening on the still-damp leaves and on the ground told her he had already finished watering the plants and trees out in front. A task she wouldn't need to see to before going home that evening.

Because that was usually the last task to be seen to at the day's end, it also meant Logan was more than likely in her daddy's office starting on closing things out.

Pulling into her usual parking spot beside the house, she cut the engine. Then she reached over to the passenger seat for her purse and jacket. Grabbing a tissue from one of the bag's side pockets, she dabbed at the tracks of moisture that ran down her cheeks. A light tap on the driver's-side window had her shooting upright with a startled gasp.

"Logan," she breathed in relief as she turned to find him smiling at her through the window, yet her heart continued at its frantic pace.

He opened the door for her. "Thought I'd catch you before you went inside to grab a sandwich or something to eat while you work this evening."

"You don't want me to eat?"

"Not here," he said. "You and I have dinner plans."

"We what?" she replied as she stepped down from the truck.

"Audra invited us to join them for dinner tonight," he explained. "Carter's whole crew as well as Nathan, Alyssa and little Katie."

"Logan…" she began, knowing it would be best for both of them to refuse.

"It's not a date," he promptly assured her as he walked her to the front porch. "Audra's making me dinner in exchange for services rendered. At least, services that will be rendered as soon as I leave here. I've gotta run by my place and load up my power auger and post diggers before I head out to their place. I'm gonna be helping Carter plant the half-dozen trees Audra bought from the nursery today."

"A half dozen?"

He nodded. "She wanted some shade trees for their front yard. Decided on a couple of Texas red oaks, a Mexican Sycamore and three pecan trees, which means unlimited pecan pies for my brother in the near future. Happy man he is."

Had she ever made Logan a pecan pie when they were dating? Not that Hope could recollect. Maybe it was the somewhat melancholy mood she was in, but the thought of never having done that for Logan made her sad.

"I offered to plant them for her if she cooked me dinner," he continued, unaware of the emotional tempest going on inside her head.

"And where do I fit into this scenario?" she asked warily.

One side of his mouth quirked up higher. That charming Cooper grin making her pulse kick up a notch. This was the side of Logan she'd missed so much. Happy. Easygoing. Genuinely sweet. "Your invite came with no strings attached. All you've gotta do is show up. You're welcome to ride with me, but then you'd be stuck watching me and Carter dig until dinner."

She used to love watching the Cooper boys work together. Granted, they were hard workers, but they always seemed to have fun doing whatever it was they were doing. But things were different now and she wasn't some teenage girl so head over heels in love with a guy that even his digging dirt could hold her attention for hours on end. She was an adult with adult responsibilities and commitments. Besides, she knew how protective the Cooper boys were of each other. She had a feeling she was the last person Nathan and Carter would want to see their brother with.

Stopping at the foot of the porch steps, she

turned to look up at him. "It's been a long day and I still have work here that needs to be taken care of. But please thank your sister-in-law for the invitation."

"If you're referring to closing out the books for today, already done."

"You didn't have to do that," she said.

"Had some free time."

"Logan," she said in frustration.

He simply smiled.

"I can't do it," she groaned. "What your family must think of me…"

"They think you're Jack's daughter and that you need looking after while he's not able to do so himself. Besides," he said, "I think you could use a good home-cooked meal."

Her gaze slid down over her naturally slender form. Had she lost weight since coming to Braxton? Food wasn't something that took much precedence in her life. She had never been a stress eater, and eating for her had become merely a source of nourishment, not pleasure.

Logan's husky chuckle drew her gaze back up to his grinning face. "Don't even go there, little darlin'. You're every bit as perfect as you ever were. Maybe even more so. However, I was referring to your eating nothing but hospital food since coming home. Other than the scant pickings you've been eating when you close out the nursery's books every evening."

Little darlin'. It felt as though he'd meant to say that, the endearment he'd given her so long ago effectively weakening her resolve. "I really shouldn't." But truth be told, she missed being a part of the Cooper fold. Being treated like one of their family. Of belonging.

"But you're gonna," he said confidently. "And you won't even have to sit by me at the table. Got myself a couple of little darlin's who've already staked their claim."

Her mood plummeted. "You're bringing two dates to dinner?"

Laughter rumbled in his broad chest. "Not exactly, and definitely not in the way you're thinking."

"I don't understand."

"Well, you see, Lily lives there. She's Audra's little girl. And Katie is coming with Nathan." His mouth quirked as he added, "My nieces are the ones who've claimed me for dinner."

His nieces. She struggled not to let her relief at his explanation show, but one look into those incredibly blue eyes of his told her she had failed miserably. Looking away, Hope fumbled with her daddy's keys to find the one to the front door. "I don't have time to make anything to bring to dinner."

"Bring yourself," he replied. "That's enough."

She looked up at him again, his large frame once again towering over her. "If you're sure my being there won't be a problem for you…"

"Not in the least."

She wasn't so sure whether to take that as a good thing or a bad thing, but smiled up at him anyway. "Then I accept Audra's invitation."

"Glad to hear it."

"On one condition," she added, a mischievous glint in her eyes.

His brows drew together. "Why didn't I guess there would be a catch? You'll go if I don't go?"

Hurt moved through her with his remark and she had no one to blame for it but herself. She had made him feel that way. While she'd had her reasons, she didn't want him to feel as though she couldn't bear to be around him. "Of course you'll be there," she said, forcing her smile back into place. "The condition is that I'm gonna help plant Audra's trees."

Surprise moved over his face. "Planting can be a dirty job."

She snorted. "You do realize who you're talking to, don't you? I grew up helping my daddy run a nursery. I've dug holes before. Besides, Daddy would have insisted on helping you boys if he was well and you know it. I'm simply doing what he would've if he were able to."

His brows knitted together. "But—"

"That's my deal," she said, cutting him off. "Take it or leave it. So am I joining you and your family for dinner tonight or not?"

"You always were stubborn," he said, shaking his head. Then, with a resigned sigh, said, "Best wear something old and bring a change of clothes along with you. Just in case."

"I plan on it," she said, starting up the steps.

"I'll be back to pick you up," he called after her.

Hope stopped and swung around to face him. "What?"

"If you're gonna join in the planting, then we're gonna be driving out to my brother's place together," he countered determinedly.

Joining him for dinner surrounded by plenty of other people was one thing, but riding with him in his truck, just the two of them in that confined space would be pure torture.

As if expecting her coming refusal, Logan said, "That's my deal, little darlin'. Take it or leave it."

"Thirsty?"

Hope paused in shoveling dirt onto the base of the newly planted pecan tree in front of her and turned to find Audra standing there, holding out a bottle of spring water. "Yes, thank you." Her gaze drifted off to the far side of the yard where Logan and Carter were digging the remaining holes for the two trees that had yet to be planted.

"I wish you and Alyssa hadn't insisted on helping Carter and the boys plant the trees," Logan's sister-in-law said as she looked past Hope to where Nathan and Alyssa were laughing happily as they worked together to fill dirt in around one of the trees near the white picket fence that ran across the expansive front yard. "You're supposed to be our guests."

Alyssa had insisted on helping Nathan when she found out that Hope was going to be lending a hand. Hope had no doubt Audra would have been digging, too, if she'd had her way. But Carter had insisted his wife take it easy, being at the end of her pregnancy and all. So Audra had settled herself on the front porch swing where she'd been keeping an eye on the children who were now playing fetch in the side yard with Mason and Lily's dog Boone and Katie's rambunctious little pup, Mistletoe.

Hope smiled. "It shouldn't take long with the five of us. Good choices, by the way."

"Thank you," Audra said, shifting the basket of chilled water bottles she'd brought out with her from the house to her other arm. "I had a nice selection to choose from."

"Daddy prides himself on the variety of plants and trees he has available for his customers," Hope said as she lowered the shovel she'd been using onto the ground beside her. Twisting the lid off the bottle of water Audra had given her, she took several long swallows.

"Your father has always been so welcoming and kind to my children and me," Audra said, absently smoothing a hand down over her swollen stomach. "Please let him know that we've been keeping him in our prayers since we heard about his being admitted to the hospital."

"I will," she nodded, knowing he would appreciate their prayers. Even if Hope herself had ceased turning to the Lord in her times of need.

Giggles filled the air, drawing their gazes in the children's direction. Logan had apparently taken a break from digging to toss Mason over his shoulder like a sack of potatoes. She watched as he raced around the yard with Audra's son, the little boy's laughter trailing behind him. Katie, Lily and the two barking pups chased after them. The scene before her both warming her heart and breaking it all at the same time.

"He's so good with children," Audra said with a warm smile as she watched her brother-in-law playing with the giggling little ones.

Hope watched him with longing. There was

so much joy on his face at that moment. Joy she hadn't been able to give him. Logan was, without a doubt, a man put on this earth to have children. Children that should have been theirs. "He always was," she said, a deep sadness filling her. In a perfect world, they would have had children of their own by now. Oh, how she longed to be carrying a child inside her just as Carter's wife was now.

Audra looked her way. "Can I ask you something?"

Hope forced her attention back to Logan's kindhearted sister-in-law. Nodding, she screwed the lid back onto the plastic water bottle and waited. Anything to distract her from the happiness she could never give Logan.

"It's personal, so please feel free to tell me to mind my own business," Audra said.

She had known it was inevitable when she'd agreed to come to dinner that someone was going to bring up her past with Logan. Demand to know why she'd treated him so poorly. Only she'd expected it to be Carter or Nathan. Not Audra or Alyssa.

"I'll try to answer if I can," Hope said, her gaze drifting once more in Logan's direction.

"Why are you so determined to avoid Logan every time you come home to visit when you're clearly still in love with him?"

Her gaze snapped back to the very pregnant woman in front of her, meeting those questioning honey-colored eyes. "Excuse me?"

"I've been watching the both of you from the porch and there was no missing the way the two of you look at each other when you think the other one isn't looking."

Logan had been watching her? It was all she could do not to look his way again. Audra had seen more than Hope was comfortable with as it was.

"Like I said, you don't have to answer that." Color filled her cheeks. "It's not really any of my business. I just care very much about my brother-in-law's happiness."

She met the other woman's worried gaze. "It's all right. I'm glad he has you to look out for him."

"And you?" she asked, her expression one of concern. "Who looks out for you?"

"I look out for myself," she answered honestly, her gaze drawn once more to the yard and the playful antics still going on between Logan and the children. Emotion constricted her throat, making it hard to breathe. "I can never be the woman Logan needs to find the happiness he's searching for," she said, her heart aching. "That's why I had to let him go."

Audra studied her for a long moment. "Maybe

not," she agreed. "But people can change. Maybe those things you thought he needed when the two of you were younger aren't the same things that are truly important to him now."

Just seeing Logan with the children was proof enough that nothing had changed. She turned her focus back to Audra and managed a smile, despite the emotional pain she felt inside. "If I can go back to San Diego knowing Logan and I can at least be friends, it would be more than I had ever thought to hope for."

Audra's gentle smile widened. "I think there's a very good possibility of that happening. You see, sometimes life takes an unexpected turn and changes everything, sending us on a whole new path. Take my life, for instance.

"I never thought I'd find love again after my first marriage ended so painfully. Mostly because I blamed myself for being the one to seek a divorce from my husband, even though it was him who had abandoned us both emotionally and physically. Yet, in my mind, I had failed God.

"I had made vows before Him. Vows I was eventually forced to break for the sake of my children. I know now that everything happens for a reason. God had a plan for me, guiding me down a path that eventually led me to find the love of my life."

Hope hadn't known any of this. Then again, her daddy was her only link to Braxton and those she'd left behind. She appreciated Audra's willingness to share a part of her painful past with her. Talking about it couldn't be easy for her.

"Weren't you angry with God for allowing the bad into your life?" Hope asked, feeling as though Audra, of all people, would understand.

"No," Audra answered sincerely. "I've come to realize that bad things are going to happen in life. It's how we choose to deal with them and the faith we cling to during those troubled times that keeps us strong and helps us to go on."

Her seeking gaze found Carter, and her smile softened. "I thank God every day for bringing Carter into my life. When my daughter drowned and had to be revived in the pond that sits behind our house last year, the Lord heard my prayers. He sent me Carter, who had been trained in CPR, a man determined not to give up on bringing Lily back to us, and through God's good grace he was able to do so."

She turned back to Hope with tears glistening in her eyes. "All you and I can do is make the best decisions we can with whatever life throws our way and have faith that the Lord has a plan for us." With a sniffle, she wiped her eyes. "I'm sorry. I don't mean to be so emotional."

"I'm sure the memory of nearly losing your child can do that," Hope said compassionately. "And since you've been so open with me, I feel I owe you the same. Ending things between Logan and me was the best decision I could make at the time." Even as she spoke the words, that sliver of doubt that had always plagued her returned. Had it truly been the best decision? Or had there been some other way?

She shook the thought from her mind. It was too late to change the past. She had to believe what she'd done was for the best, no matter how painful it had been for all of those involved. "Loving someone sometimes means letting them go." She felt the need to explain. Just as she'd had to do when her momma died. She had let Logan go because she loved him so deeply.

As if sensing he was being watched, Logan glanced her way from across the yard. His tanned face split into a wide smile that set her heart aflutter.

"Would you make that same decision today?" Audra asked beside her.

Hope let her gaze drop to the shovel by her feet. "Yes," she said with a sorrowful sigh. "Nothing's changed."

"Then I will pray for the two of you to find your way back to, at the very least, a comfortable friendship. And if you ever feel the need to talk, you know where to find me," Audra offered before walking away to distribute water to the others.

Talking was something Hope preferred not to do, because there were times when the truth was better off left unsaid. She didn't want anyone's pity. And she especially didn't want Logan to sacrifice the happiness he deserved, the children he longed for, because he felt he needed to do the right thing by trying to love her in spite of her inability to give him a family.

A little under two hours after they'd begun, the tree planting was complete and everyone had washed up for dinner. The entire group was now seated around a large rectangular table eating the homemade lasagna Audra had baked for dinner. Though her thoughts had been troubled since speaking with Audra earlier, Hope soon relaxed and fell into the busy conversation going on around the dinner table.

She couldn't help but smile as she eyed the men's plates. One thing that hadn't changed as the Cooper boys had grown into big, strong men was their appetites. Their plates were piled high with lasagna and garlic bread. If she even so much as thought about eating that much food it would have gone straight to her waist. But not in their case. The three Cooper boys had grown into veritable giants without an ounce of fat on them.

"You have pretty hair," Lily announced from across the dinner table.

It took Hope a moment to realize Audra's little girl was talking to her. Smiling appreciatively, she said, "Thank you, Lily. So do you."

"But mine doesn't look like the sky when it's getting ready for bed," the four-year-old replied with a sigh.

"That would be sunset, sweetie," Audra clarified for her young daughter.

Hope had never received such a lovely compliment. "My hair might look like a sleepy sky, Lily, but my eyes don't have flecks of gold dust sparkling in them like yours do. They're very pretty."

Lily's eyes lit up with the compliment, making them sparkle even brighter. "My mommy gave them to me."

"That was very nice of her." Hope looked to Katie. "And those curls of yours are just beautiful. I wish mine were as full and bouncy as yours."

"I have boy hair," Mason said, sounding disappointed.

Hope laughed softly. "But look at those muscles. I swear they're nearly as big as your uncle Logan's."

Carter snorted, nearly choking on the drink of lemonade he'd just taken.

Nathan gave Logan a playful jab in the side. "Best start looking into a gym membership."

Audra's son looked on in confusion at the playful ribbing Carter and Nathan were giving their younger brother.

Alyssa shot her fiancé a quelling look before redirecting her gaze to Mason. "Hope's right," she told him. "You do have some pretty impressive muscles. And, while they're not quite as large as your uncle Logan's, they're definitely bigger than your uncle Nathan's."

Logan released a husky chuckle as his future sister-in-law came to his defense. "I do like this girl you're fixing to marry, Nathan. If you happen to change your mind about marrying her, can I have her?"

Hope felt a tug of yearning in her heart. Teasing or not, she didn't want to listen to Logan talk about wanting another woman. And this was only Alyssa, the woman his brother loved and would be marrying in the next month. What if he'd been saying such things, even playfully, about a woman who would be free to return Logan's feelings?

One day soon, that would happen. All she could think of was that it was a good thing she'd turned her daddy's offer down. She couldn't bear to live here in Braxton and watch the man she loved fall in love with, and someday marry, someone else.

Katie giggled. "You can't have her, Uncle Logan. She's my daddy's."

"Katie's right," Nathan replied with a grin. "She's mine. Find your own girl."

Logan shrugged his broad shoulders and then reached out to pluck a slice of garlic bread from the cloth-lined basket in front of him. "No surprise there. I already figured as much."

"Gotta watch him," Carter warned Nathan. "Why do you think I married my gal so quick?"

"And here I thought it was because you had fallen madly in love with me at first sight," Audra joined in with a feigned pout. "And now I find out it was simply to beat your brother to the punch."

"Darlin', need I remind you that first sight for me was a pair of legs dangling precariously from a sagging porch roof. One flip-flop on. The other lying on the ground by the bushes."

"Carter," she groaned, her cheeks pinkening at the teasing reminder.

With a chuckle, Carter leaned in to curl an arm around his wife's slender shoulders. "Truth is there isn't a man alive who's more crazy about his wife than this man here."

"That's because Alyssa and I aren't married yet," Nathan muttered between chews.

Hope could feel the love in the room, surrounding her. *This* was the life she had given up when she'd broken Logan's heart all those years ago. A life she yearned for, but would never truly be a part of.

Chapter Seven

The sound of a vehicle coming up the drive that led to Hope's Garden had Logan turning from the bags of mulch he'd been stacking. Dragging the sleeve of his flannel shirt across his brow, he stepped from between two of the greenhouses, assuming it was another customer.

To his surprise, he saw that it was Hope in her daddy's truck. Raising a gloved hand, he waved to her, but her gaze never strayed in his direction. Instead, she went right on by the main nursery building to the house far behind it.

The faster-than-normal speed in which she'd driven past, combined with the fact that she was home at lunchtime when she always ate her meal with her daddy at the hospital, gave Logan cause to worry. Had something happened to Jack?

Pulling off the dirt-covered work gloves, he tossed them onto a nearby wooden worktable and broke into a run, cutting through the scattered nursery buildings to Jack's place out back.

Hope was already out of the truck and in the house by the time Logan got there, deepening his concern. Saying a quick prayer to the Lord to keep Jack firmly embraced in His healing arms, he shot up onto the porch, taking the steps two at a time. Whipping open the screen door, he hollered from where he stood in the open doorway, "Hope?"

"In the kitchen," she called back, her voice somewhat muffled. Was she crying? Lord, he hoped not. If something had happened, she would have called him from the hospital. Wouldn't she?

He moved through the house with the ease of someone who had spent a lot of time in it, which he had. Both when he'd been dating Hope and then when he'd paid visits to Jack after she'd moved away from Braxton.

His hurried strides took him into the kitchen where his worried gaze slid over to the open refrigerator. Hope stood behind the open door, determinedly rooting through the fridge shelves.

Muttering to herself, she straightened and then turned to place a jar of dill pickles onto the kitchen counter beside her. An unopened package of bacon strips followed.

Logan raised a brow as he watched, his concern ebbing. A grin tugged at his lips. This was the last thing he'd expected to find Hope doing when she'd come barreling up the drive the way she had.

"They run out of food at the hospital?" he teased, now that he knew everything was okay. If something had happened with Jack, a fridge raid would be the last thing Hope would be doing right then.

She paused in her endeavor and turned to look up at him, a wayward coppery curl hanging down over her face. She blew out a puff of air, which only lifted the silken spiral for a moment before it settled back onto her pert little nose.

With a chuckle, Logan stepped forward and pushed the curly tendril back into place. "I see some things never change. That pretty hair of yours still has a mind of its own."

Eyes the color of grass in early spring looked up at him, softening. The way she used to look up at him when they were two young kids who fancied themselves in love.

Hope was the first to break away, tucking herself between the open refrigerator door and the contents inside. "Some days it tends to be far less manageable than others. And, to answer your question, I didn't come home to eat. I came home to clean out Daddy's fridge." Explanation made, she went back to doing just that.

He moved to lean against the counter beside her, arms folded, boots crossed casually at the ankle. "Any particular reason you're cleaning out Jack's fridge in the middle of the afternoon?"

"Because he's coming home," she replied as she continued pulling items from the fridge.

His expression grew serious. "They're letting Jack out?"

She glanced back over her shoulder at him with a joyous smile. "Later this afternoon, once his doctor releases him and the paperwork is completed."

"Glad to hear it. He'll be much happier in his own bed."

"As if I'll have much success keeping him in it," she muttered with a shake of her head. "You know Daddy."

"You've got a point. We'll just have to make sure he doesn't overdo things when he's up and about."

She stood, her expression growing serious. "Logan, I want you to know how much I appreciate all you've done for him. And for caring. I'm glad he has you here to keep an eye on him."

"I take it this means you'll be leaving soon."

"Not right away," she replied, her words easing some of the tension that slid through him the moment she'd told him Jack was coming home. "I wanna be here when he starts physical therapy for his arm, to make sure he's doing all right."

He would much rather Jack didn't have to go through therapy, but Logan had to admit he was grateful for the chance to spend some extra time with Hope before she went back to San Diego. Because he was nowhere near ready for her to leave. Not when he'd made the much-thought-over decision to forgive her. To see if there was any chance for this new friendship they had formed to grow into something more. Hope wasn't the only one who missed what they'd once shared.

His gaze shifted to the growing stack of food atop the kitchen counter and then back to Hope. "So you got the news that your daddy's gonna be coming home and decided to clean out the fridge?"

She laughed softly. "I suppose you could look at it that way. Daddy needs to start taking better care of himself," she explained as she pulled a package of deli meat from the meat and cheese drawer. "That means eating better than he has been. So I picked up some groceries on the way home to replace all of the unhealthy food choices he has in here." She added the disposable plastic storage container of sliced smoked turkey breast to the growing pile of food on the counter.

"Turkey's not healthy?"

"Not when it comes in the form of packaged cold cuts," she said as she stepped past him to grab a kitchen trash bag from under the sink. "Packaged meats are full of sodium. As are pickles and bacon and so many things most folks take for granted until blood pressure issues arise." Shaking out the garbage bag to open it, she began tossing the discarded contents from the fridge into it.

He nodded toward the bag. "What are you gonna do with all that food?"

"I'm getting rid of it," she replied matter-of-factly. "Daddy doesn't need to be tempted by it."

"No sense wasting it," he muttered, not wanting to see good food wasted. "I'll take it home with me."

She gasped. "You most certainly will not. I'm not about to contribute to your eating something that isn't good for you. I couldn't bear it if…" She snapped her mouth shut.

"If something happened to me?" he prodded with a teasing grin.

"Don't you have plants to water or something?" she grumbled as she went back to disposing the salt-laden foods.

"As a matter of fact I do," he replied, pushing away from the counter. "When I saw you come up the drive faster than normal, I was worried something had happened with Jack. So I dropped everything and hightailed it after you to find out what was wrong. Now that I know everything's all right, better than all right," he added with a smile, "I'll be heading back."

She returned his smile. "Thank you for your concern."

"When you're done raiding the fridge, can you stop in at the nursery? There's something I wanna talk to you about."

"I'm not sure I can spare the time right now," she said. "I wanna return to the hospital as soon as I'm done here in case they release him sooner than expected."

Her words brought him back to that evening he'd driven her home after having lasagna at his brother's place. Dinner, as well as the time they'd spent planting Audra's trees, had gone even better than he'd expected. It was as if the old Hope was back. Then something changed near the end of dinner and she withdrew emotionally. Not from the others, but from him.

She barely spoke a word their entire drive home. When he'd asked if she wanted to take a ride on into town to get a shake, maybe talk a little, she'd told him she didn't think she could spare the time. That she had things to do before turning in for the night. So he'd spent most of that same night unable to sleep, trying to figure out what he had done, or said, wrong to cause her to shut him out again.

Logan nodded. "Understandable." He preferred to talk to her before Jack came home, but apparently that wasn't going to happen. Maybe it was for the best, he decided. Hope had enough on her plate as it was. He could take care of this situation Jack had somehow gotten himself into. "It can wait," he told her. "See you later."

"See you."

He strode from the kitchen, his concerns regarding the nursery weighing heavily on his mind. Hope had mentioned something to him a couple of days before about needing to take care of a couple of past due utility bills. She'd said that Jack's higher-than-normal blood pressure had affected his ability to focus, which had resulted in a few things getting overlooked.

More than a few it seemed. Two calls had come in that morning in regards to orders that he could find no record of, which he'd then scrambled to pull together. Then a supplier left a message on the answering machine, canceling a follow-up delivery they were waiting on due to non-payment on the first order. Fortunately, when Logan called them back and explained the situation, the man he'd spoken to had agreed to put the delivery back onto their schedule if payment was made over the phone for the complete order. Logan had taken care of it, using his own credit card.

He stepped between two of the greenhouses, making his way to the front of the buildings. Hope needed to know what was going on, yet he hesitated being the bearer of bad news once again. She had turned down her daddy's offer to take over the business. Maybe this was something he needed to handle on his own. At least until Jack was back on his feet and could see to things again. He had no doubt the man would settle any debts Logan incurred, righting things for him. So what was the right thing to do? Tell Hope or keep the information between him and Jack?

Torn over what to do, Logan turned to the Lord in prayer. "Lord, I ask of You to give me the wisdom and the ability to turn things around for my good friend. This place," he said, looking around, "means the world to him. I'd rather not let him down like I somehow let his daughter down a long time ago."

Rounding the front of the main building, he stepped inside and made his way back to the office. Taking a seat at the desk, he reached out to press the play button on the answering machine, making a note of anything important, and of calls that needed to be returned. Then he began going through that day's mail.

"Figured if you couldn't make time to come by the bowling alley to see me, I'd come to you."

Logan glanced up from the envelope he'd been opening to see his best friend, Ryan, standing in the office doorway. A slow smile spread across his face. "Feeling needy today?"

Ryan strode into the room. "If I were, there'd be prettier faces I could be looking at than yours."

"Like Lizzie's?"

His friend dropped down into the old slat-back chair beside Jack's desk. "I was thinking more along the line of Doris and Myrna Wilson's. Those two serve a mean cup of tea and the best cookies around. And they're more than happy to listen to a man's woes. Unlike some people, and I'll refrain from pointing an accusing finger in your direction, who don't even know which end of the tea bag goes into the cup, can't bake a lick and are too wrapped up helping a pretty female to make time for his best friend."

He had to admit, Doris and Myrna did have him beat in the tea-making and cookie-baking department. The elderly sisters had hearts of gold and loved to entertain guests at their boardinghouse. Logan leaned back against the desk chair, folding his arms behind his head. "Okay, so if you're not here to share a cup of tea, or in this case some incredibly rank coffee," he added, lifting his coffee cup, "then what really brings you all the way out here?"

"Confession forthcoming," his friend warned, his expression growing serious. "I've been worried about you."

"About me?"

Ryan nodded. "I know how close you and Jack are. And then with Hope back in town and the two of you having to cross paths daily...well, I wasn't sure how you were holding up."

"Better than expected," Logan assured him. "For the first time in nine years, Hope and I have been able to remain in close proximity to each other without her running off." He stood and crossed the room to top off his half-empty cup of coffee. "We even had dinner at Carter's the other evening."

"You asked her to dinner?"

"Not exactly," he admitted. "Audra invited her. I accompanied her there."

"I didn't realize Audra knew Hope," Ryan said in confusion.

"She was at the nursery buying some shade trees for their front yard and extended the invite. Insisted actually, leaving it up to me to convince Hope to join them."

"I'll bet Carter loved that," Ryan said, knowing how Logan's brothers felt about the way

Hope had treated their baby brother when she'd ended things between them.

"Audra has a way of calming the waters," Logan said. Then he went on to tell his friend about that evening and how well Hope had gotten along with Audra and Alyssa and, more important, the children.

"I'm not the least bit surprised to hear Hope managed to endear herself with the children. She always had a way with little ones when we were growing up. Truth is I expected her to have a bundle of her own by now. The way she always used to talk about wanting several so they wouldn't have to grow up an only child like she had."

Logan thought he'd have a bundle of children, too, by now. But marriage didn't seem to be in the cards for him. Was it for Hope? Did she have someone special back in San Diego she intended to create that family with? The thought of it had him frowning.

"I'm sorry," Ryan apologized. "I shouldn't have brought that up. I know there was a time when you thought you'd be the one having children with Hope."

"Apparently, the Lord has other plans for me," he said. Then, holding up the steaming mug of coffee, asked, "Sure I can't pour you a cup?"

Ryan waved the offer away. "I'm good. Already had my fill of coffee at Big Dog's before coming out here."

Logan arched a brow. "Big Dog's, huh? That means it must be Lizzie's early workday."

"Lizzie has nothing to do with my wanting something other than cold cereal in the morning every once in a while. It's the breakfast platter special Verna offers that lures this man in."

Logan wasn't so sure he believed that was the only reason for Ryan's stopping by the diner, but he had to admit Verna was the best cook around. Not that Wyatt was all too bad of a cook himself. He was Verna's nephew and helped her out in the kitchen part-time during evenings and weekends. Their specialty breakfast platter was a big draw, served heaped full of eggs and bacon with a side of homemade biscuits and sausage gravy.

"Anything new in town?" he asked as he returned to the chair behind the desk.

"No, but I have other news," his friend replied.

"Must be good, considering the smile that just moved across your face."

He nodded. "It is. Hayden's coming home for Nathan's wedding and she's bringing the baby with her."

Hayden was Ryan's younger sister. She and Lizzie had been best friends all through high school. After high school, Hayden had gone off to college, met the love of her life and married him. They were currently living at Camp Lejeune, NC, where her husband, J.D., a US Marine, was stationed.

"Baby," Logan said, shaking his head. "I still can't wrap my head around the fact that your little sister has a baby of her own now." He couldn't help but envy J.D. for the blessing he'd been given. A child. Something he himself longed for. A large family of his own. A chance to become the kind of father his own daddy had been. He'd like to think that maybe someday…but his heart had already been given away. And he wouldn't want to bring children into a house not filled with the same depth of love and joy as his own home had been when he was growing up.

"Now remember you promised me not to overdo things when you get home," Hope said to her daddy as they neared Braxton.

"I'll do my best, sugar," he replied as his gaze drifted to the passing scenery outside the passenger window.

Her daddy looked so much healthier. The color had returned to his face. He looked better rested, despite his complaints about being awakened through the night by the nurses who were probably more anxious to get him out of there than he was to go. He'd so much as admitted he made a terrible patient.

"Is there anything you'd like for me to get for you while we're in town?"

He looked her way. "Well, since you're asking…"

Five minutes later Hope was pulling up in front of Big Dog's. "I don't think this is a very good idea," she muttered worriedly. "You need to be home relaxing in your recliner."

"A man can't heal without nourishment," he replied as he undid his seat belt. "I was on the verge of wasting away in that hospital. Sugar-free JELL-O. Yogurt. Broiled fish." He rolled his eyes. "This is Texas. Fry that fish in some seasoned bread crumbs and real butter. Better yet, give me a slab of roast beef with a side of mashed potatoes smothered in homemade gravy."

"I agreed to bring you here on one condition," Hope reminded him. "No fried food." And to think she'd been worried about his being up and about for too long. It was his poor eating habits she needed to concern herself over.

"Gravy isn't fried," he said with a teasing grin as he opened the door and stepped out of the truck.

How was she ever going to leave her daddy

to fend for himself? She'd been sitting right there with him when the dietitian went over the dietary changes he needed to make to help keep his blood pressure down. Yet, none of it seemed to have registered.

With a groan, Hope hurried to undo her seat belt and then grabbed for her purse before stepping out of the truck.

"Daddy," she said as she joined him where he stood waiting for her just outside of the diner.

"Yes, honey?"

"Don't forget to watch your salt intake."

"One shake instead of two from the salt-shaker from now on," he promised with a grin as he pulled open the diner door and motioned her inside. "You have my word."

"Well, look who we have here," Lizzie said, her smile warm and welcoming. "Welcome home, Mr. Dillan."

"Thank you, Lizzie. Good to be back."

"Verna is gonna be tickled pink to know you finally got released from that there hospital. She's been fretting up a storm since they admitted you to County General."

"That woman frets over everything," Jack grumbled, but his tone said he really didn't mind all the fussing over him Verna Simms did. "Reckon you'd best let her know I'm here. To put her mind at ease and all."

"I'll do that," Lizzie said. "Grab a seat. I'll fetch some menus." That said, she scurried off through the crimson-colored door that divided the front of the diner from the kitchen.

"Table or booth?" her daddy asked.

"Either's fine with me," Hope replied.

With a nod, he chose a table close to the back of the room. Her daddy seemed eager and anxious all at the same time as he settled onto one of the four chairs that hugged up against the small round table, his gaze fixed on the dark red door.

"You feeling all right?" she asked worriedly, finding his behavior a bit off as he pulled a small black comb from the back pocket of his jeans and made a quick pass through his hair with it.

Jack Dillan was not one to fuss over his appearance. Probably because he never really went anywhere except for church, and on occasion into town for some shopping or a bite to eat.

But sure enough, he was fussing. Tucking the comb away, his fingers moved to the collar of his shirt, making certain it was lying just right.

Before she could question his strange behavior, the door he'd been watching swung open and Verna shot out through it in a fluster of squeals. "Jack! You're home!" she exclaimed. "Thank the good Lord above."

"Not quite *home*," he replied with a grin. "But the next best thing to it."

Since when did Big Dog's become her daddy's next best thing to home? What happened to the nursery in the placement of things in his life?

"I wanted to stop by on my way home to say hello," her daddy went on, drawing Hope's attention back to the conversation going on in front of her.

To say hello? What happened to wanting to stop by the diner because he was wasting away from the not-as-good-as-homemade hospital food he'd been eating?

Hope looked from her daddy's widening grin to Verna's bright-eyed smile and then back again. Realization hit her like a ton of bricks. How had she not seen it before? Verna was always bringing him soup and other fixings. Her daddy was always complaining halfheartedly about the widow's fussing over him. Jack Dillan was smitten.

It shouldn't surprise her. He'd been alone for a very long time. But she couldn't help but feel a little hurt that he'd kept his feelings for Verna from her. Did he think she would be upset if she found out? If so, he was wrong. She knew how much he loved her momma. But life could be very lonely when one was living it alone. She knew that for a fact. More than anything, she wanted him to be healthy and happy. It appeared they needed to have a very serious father-daughter talk when they got home.

"I'll bet you're glad to have your daddy home again," Verna said, turning to Hope.

"Very much so," she replied. "Now if I can just get him to follow his doctor's orders."

"After five days in that hospital, you don't have to worry about my not doing what I'm supposed to be doing," he said determinedly.

"Glad to hear it," Verna said.

Lizzie swung by with the menus. "Just give me a holler when you're ready to order."

"We will," Hope replied, reaching for one of the menus.

"Will I be seeing you at church services on Sunday?"

Hope's gaze lifted over the top of the menu she'd just opened. She was just about to tell Verna not to expect her, when she realized the older woman hadn't been speaking to her.

Her daddy nodded. "You can count on it. I've got a few things to be thanking the good Lord for."

"Daddy," Hope said, lowering the menu, "you're not supposed to be driving yet. You heard the doctor."

The decision as to whether or not she would need to take a leave of absence from her job had been made for her that afternoon when the nurse was going over his restrictions. One of those being a thirty-day wait until he could drive again.

She had to remember to call her office in the morning and make the necessary arrangements for the time off she was going to require. One good thing to come from her having no personal life. All she did was work, which meant she had plenty of vacation time saved up to put toward caring for her daddy.

"Not sure why not," he grumbled in response to the reminder. "I still got one good driving arm. And church is days away."

"Daddy…"

With a chuckle, he looked to Verna. "She's an even bigger fusser than you are."

"Well, you best consider yourself a blessed man," she told him, not the least bit offended by his teasing comment. "It's fussy females like us who see to it that stubborn men like you take proper care of yourselves. So instead of belly-aching about it, I suggest you try appreciating it." She sent a conspiratorial wink in Hope's direction.

"You know what, Verna?" he said, sitting back against the diner chair. "You're right."

"I am?" she said, seemingly surprised by his response.

"I do need to appreciate things more in my life." He looked to Hope. "Like the time we have together before you go back to San Diego." Then he swung his gaze back to Verna. "Hope will be driving me to church this Sunday. That way she and I can spend more time together before she's busy seeing to the nursery and I'm stuck recuperating back at the house."

She was going to do what? Her driving him to church had never come up in any of their discussions. And, if it was up to her, it never would have.

Verna smiled. "Well, then, I look forward to seeing the both of you at Sunday services. It'll be just like old times, having Hope there to join us in worship."

Hope felt trapped. Church was the last place she wanted to be. But she couldn't back out without raising questions she'd prefer not to have to answer. So she pasted on a happy face and said, "Just like old times."

Lizzie walked over to their table. "Are you ready to order?"

"I'll have the usual," her daddy said.

"Make that a salad," Verna told Lizzie, overriding his decision. "With light Italian dressing."

He quirked a brow. "Now hold on a minute."

Verna folded her arms and tipped her head ever so slightly. "Yes?"

He sighed. "Can I at least have some chicken in it?"

Verna looked to Lizzie. "Grilled not fried." Then she swung her gaze around in Hope's direction. "And for you?"

It was all Hope could do not to laugh. Verna wasn't about to let her daddy do anything less than take the very best care of himself. "That actually sounds really good. Make that two grilled chicken salads with light Italian."

"Well, then, I'd best get myself back to the kitchen so Wyatt and I can get started on those salads," Verna announced. Then, with a sweet smile aimed specifically at Jack Dillan, she said, "You listen to your little girl and take care of yourself. I'll see you in a few days."

"Sooner if I happen to venture into town for lunch," he replied, his tone almost tender.

Hope looked to see if Lizzie noticed the overly warm exchange between her daddy and Verna, but the younger woman gave no sign of picking up on anything unusual as she gathered up the menus.

"Verna," her daddy called out as she started for the kitchen.

She stopped and turned to look at him. "Yes?"

"I was wondering if you were gonna be going to Nathan and Alyssa's wedding."

"I wouldn't miss it for the world," she replied with a bright smile. "And you?"

"Wild horses couldn't keep me away." He cleared his throat, adding almost nervously, "I hope you'll consider saving me a dance."

"Daddy," Hope groaned.

"Sugar," he cut in with tempered patience, "I got myself two good legs. Dancing won't be an issue. I'll just make certain not to overdo things."

"Tell you what," Verna said. "I'll make a deal with you. You behave yourself by following all your doctor's orders and I'll be sure to save you two dances. *Slow* dances," she added with a conspiratorial wink at Hope.

Thank you, Hope mouthed. She worried that her daddy would push himself too hard too fast. It was good to know she had Verna as an ally when it came to keeping him reined in.

"You've got yourself a deal," he replied without hesitation and then with a grin looked to Hope. "Doubt I'll be able to get away with much with my daughter looking after me for the next week or so."

"Month," Hope said after Verna had walked away. "I'll be sticking around until you're able to get yourself about again." She couldn't expect others to drive him around.

"I'd like to have you around permanently," he said. "Take over my half of the business."

Her gaze snapped up to meet his. "Your half? Does that mean Logan accepted your offer?"

"Not yet," he admitted. "But he's gonna. Only thing holding him back as far as I can tell is you."

"Me?"

"Despite everything that's gone on between the two of you, your feelings matter to him." He leaned forward, resting his bad arm on the table. "If you're set on not coming home, then I'd like for you to talk to Logan. Let him know that you're okay with him taking on part ownership of the family business, maybe even the whole thing when I get to the point I am ready to step away completely."

It surprised her to hear that Logan cared about her feelings. Why would he after all she'd put him through? Was there still a part of his heart, despite his words otherwise, that she filled? Just as he did hers? And could she find the strength to tell him it was okay when it really wasn't? Not that Logan would be a bad choice as a business partner for her daddy. Quite the opposite. He was smart and hardworking and unfailingly trustworthy.

But this was her family's business. One she longed to be a part of. To do so meant coming home, and she didn't think she could bear living in the same town as the man she loved. She knew he would inevitably fall in love and marry and then she'd have to watch from a distance as he raised the family he'd always wanted. One she would never be a part of.

Once again, she found herself in the position of having to do what was right. No matter how it would affect her emotionally.

Hope nodded her consent, despite feeling torn apart inside, and said quietly, "I'll let him know."

Chapter Eight

Hope stood looking at her reflection in the dresser mirror. Gone was the happy little girl who had grown up in Braxton. The one who had hopes and dreams and a heart filled with love.

In her place was a woman with no real direction in life. One who refused to dream about the future, because those dreams couldn't include Logan Cooper. A woman who had given up on her faith, but would that very morning be seated in the church she'd once worshipped in.

There was no backing out. She'd given her word to her daddy to take him to church and she wasn't about to let him down.

Running a hand down over the front of her dress to smooth out any wrinkles, she took a deep breath and then scooped up her purse and made her way downstairs to let her daddy know she was ready. Or as ready as she ever would be.

She found him waiting for her on the front porch, seated in one of the oversize rockers and walked over to where he sat waiting for her.

He greeted her with a loving smile. "Ready to go?"

No, she wasn't. Not even close. She felt anxious at the very thought of what lay ahead. *As ready as I'll ever be*, she felt like saying. Instead, she nodded. "I'll go get the truck."

"No need," a deep, clearly masculine voice said behind her.

She turned to find Logan standing there, one shoulder propped against the wood siding at the opposite end of the porch, booted feet crossed casually. "Logan," she said in surprise.

He grinned as he tipped his cowboy hat to her. "Hope."

"What are you doing here?"

Pushing away from the wall, he crossed the porch. "Taking you and your daddy to church."

"Logan offered," her daddy explained. "No sense in him going alone when we could join him. It'll be just like old times."

She didn't want it to be like old times. There were too many memories her attending church with Logan would stir up. She fidgeted with the purse strap she had twined around her hands. "Since you have a ride to church, I think I'll

stay home and take care of some of the paperwork at the nursery."

"Not today," her daddy said firmly. "This is
the Lord's day. Work gets placed on the back
burner. Now give me a minute to grab my Bible
and then we can get going."

She watched him go, wishing she had thought
to fetch his Bible for him. Then she wouldn't
be standing there alone with Logan and all the
emotions he tended to stir up inside her.

"You look right pretty today, little darlin',"
Logan said in a husky drawl.

Her heart skittered, just as it always did
whenever he'd called her that.

"Too pretty to be frowning," he added.
"Wanna talk about it?"

She shook her head and then lifted her gaze
to meet his. Bluer than blue eyes filled with a
hint of tenderness looked down at her. Oh, how
she wished she could. "I just have a lot on my
mind."

Logan nodded. "Reckon you do."

"And I'm not really up for church this morning."

Concern immediately replaced the tenderness
she'd seen in his eyes. "You're not feeling well?"

"I'm feeling fine," she assured him. It felt
so good to have someone other than her daddy
worry about her well-being. She cast a quick

glanced toward the door to make certain her daddy wasn't in hearing range before adding, "Church doesn't hold the same pull for me as it once did."

Logan studied her for a long moment before saying, "So you and the Lord have had a parting of ways?"

She nodded her reply, for some reason unable to say the words.

He eyed her skeptically. "I find that hard to believe." And then his expression changed. "Are you trying to avoid going to church because I'll be there? Because I thought we'd moved past some of our issues. At least enough to be in the same room together."

She wanted to tell him that it had nothing to do with him, but in a way it did. With him. With them. With all the injustices in life. She settled for, "It's not because you're gonna be there." She took a seat in the rocker her daddy had just vacated and began to rock, needing to release some of the tension she was feeling at that moment.

"Then why?" he asked, no condemnation in his tone. "What happened that turned you away from your faith?"

"Life," she replied. "And I didn't quit on the Lord first. He quit on me."

Logan settled his large frame into the rocking

chair next to hers. "Hope," he said tenderly as he covered her hand with his own, "the Lord would never abandon you. But that doesn't mean bad things can't happen. When they do, He's there for us to turn to for strength and guidance."

"I don't wanna talk about Him," she said, sliding her hand free from Logan's comforting grasp. She folded her arms across her chest and rocked harder.

He watched her for a long moment before asking, "Does this have something to do with your momma?"

The creak of the screen door as it swung open gave Hope a reprieve from the uncomfortable conversation she and Logan had been moving toward.

Her daddy stepped out onto the porch, his Bible held securely in the crook of his good arm. "Sorry to keep you two waiting. Almost forgot to take my pills."

She should have thought to remind him, something she would be sure to do until it became routine for him to take his medications again.

"You kids ready?" he asked.

Logan pushed out of the rocker and then turned to face her, holding out a hand to help her up. "You ready?"

She pasted on a smile as she took his offered hand. "Ready as I'll ever be."

"We'd best get heading, then," her daddy said as he started for the steps. "Wouldn't wanna be late."

Hope followed, feeling Logan's gaze on her as she walked away. Maybe now that he knew she no longer shared the same faith in the Lord as he did, he would stop smiling at her with such tenderness. Stop treating her like the girl he once knew and loved.

They had to work together to keep things up and running smoothly at the nursery until her daddy could take over again. But that was all. Until then, she needed to do whatever it took to keep that emotional wall up between them before she did something she would regret—like hurt Logan all over again. *Please, Lord, give me strength.*

That last thought took her aback. She didn't want to turn to the Lord in prayer. Didn't want to sit inside church while others welcomed her back. She wasn't back. Not in that sense. And she didn't want to still be in love with Logan Cooper. But as she'd long since learned, things rarely went the way she wanted them to. Especially where her heart was concerned.

Jack was right, Logan thought as he settled himself behind the wheel of his extended cab pickup. It was just like old times, with Hope wedged in between him and Jack on the bench seat. The only difference was that Jack used to be the one behind the wheel with Logan sitting against the passenger-side door. That and the worrisome knowledge that Hope no longer believed.

What could have happened to make her pull away from the Lord? Did this go back to her losing her momma? He'd thought his own momma had helped her work through that painful loss. But maybe her more recent passing had shaken Hope's faith.

Whatever the reason, Logan knew firsthand, as had been the case with his older brother, that faith could be restored. Hope just needed a little help finding her way back.

His thoughts remained on the woman seated quietly beside him as he pulled away from the house and down the long drive leading past the nursery. Only it wasn't her faltering faith he was thinking about at that moment. It was how fetching she looked this morning.

It was the first time he'd seen Hope dressed up since she'd returned to Braxton. Working at a nursery didn't call for fancy clothes. Neither did long days spent at the hospital. And while she looked fetching in anything she wore, she looked even more so today. The image of her stepping out onto the porch, the rising sun caressing her pretty face, had embedded itself in his mind.

She'd chosen a white, button-up sweater to keep her warm on that chilly March morning. The wispy skirt of the dress underneath hit just below her knees. The dress, the same shade as the clear blue sky above, complemented the stray, curling tendrils of coppery hair that had escaped the clip she'd used to pull it up. The same curls that were now subtly framing her face.

A natural beauty.

Jack cleared his throat. "Son, you might wanna get going. The light's green."

Logan snapped out of his thoughts of Hope to glance up at the traffic light above. *Come on, Cooper, pull yourself together.*

However, wanting to do something and actually doing it were two different things. He tried not to focus on Hope's nearness. Or the sweet scent of ripe berries that teased his senses. She'd always had a preference for body lotions and perfumes that were fruit-scented, saying she got her fill of floral at the nursery.

"How'd you sleep last night?" he asked Jack. Anything to take his mind off the woman seated beside him.

"Like a log," his friend replied. "Unlike my daughter who was still up pacing the floor when I finally drifted off to sleep."

Logan glanced down at her questioningly, wondering if her inability to sleep had anything to do with him. With them. Because his troubled thoughts where they were concerned had most definitely kept him from settling into any sort of peaceful slumber from the moment she'd come back to town.

Conversation ebbed after that. Jack silently watching the passing landscape outside. Hope suddenly preoccupied with a text on her cell phone. And Logan, well, he was just trying to focus on the road instead of how pretty Hope looked in her Sunday best.

Church, as was the norm, had drawn a crowd that morning. Reverend Johns always offered up sermons that were guaranteed to move you in some way.

Logan spotted both of his brothers' trucks in the parking lot and smiled. It was good having the entire family attending services again. Not just physically, but emotionally and spiritually, as well.

Like Hope, Nathan had pushed the Lord away. Right after losing Isabel. In fact, there had been a time when he and Carter feared Nathan might never find his way back to the faith he'd once known. And then Alyssa came into his life. The guiding light his brother had needed.

Logan pulled into an empty spot and cut the

engine. They had just stepped from the car when three little beaming faces came charging across the churchyard to greet them.

"Uncle Logan!" Katie hollered, her long dark curls bouncing around as she hurried toward him, her limp not slowing her down one bit.

"Uncle Logan!" Mason and Lily chimed in, as well.

All he could do was grin as the children wrapped themselves around his legs, one by one until he was completely surrounded. He chuckled. "Now that's the kind of welcome guaranteed to warm a man's heart."

"Or wrinkle his dress pants," Nathan added with a chuckle.

"I'd trade a few wrinkles for this any day," he told his brother.

"You need some kids like us, Uncle Logan," Lily told him as she craned her neck to look up at him from where she stood clinging to his pant leg.

"Maybe someday, sweet pea," he replied with a tender smile. Audra's children might not be blood related, but they filled a very special place in his heart, right alongside his beloved niece.

"Where's Miss Dillan going?" Mason asked, his gaze fixed in the direction of the church.

Logan glanced back over his shoulder to find Hope walking away. His smile sank as he noted her hurried pace and the slight bow to her slender shoulders. As if she was upset about something more than just having to attend that morning's services. But try as he might, he couldn't come up with anything that might have sent her running off.

"On into church, I reckon," he said. Maybe he was reading more into her action than there really was.

"Probably figured she'd head on inside and save us some seats," Jack muttered as he stood watching his daughter's retreating back. His graying brows were drawn together, his expression telling Logan he, too, had sensed something was off with Hope's leaving the way she had.

Carter appeared in the church's open doorway just as Hope reached the sidewalk that lined the front of the church. With a nod of greeting, he moved past her, his sight set on the children. Grinning, he crossed the churchyard, quickly closing the distance between them.

"We came to collect our little ones," Carter announced when he joined the gathering.

"You mean these aren't burrs I've got clinging to my pants?" Logan said with feigned confusion.

The children giggled.

"You know I think they might be," Jack agreed with a nod.

Carter reached down to peel Mason off Logan. "Yep," he said as he slung Audra's son over his shoulder, tickling him playfully. "A big ol' giggly burr."

"I'm thinking you'd best tickle these last two pesky burrs until they fall off me," Logan said. "I can't be taking them with me into church. They might stick to the pews. Or even the reverend's robe."

More tiny giggles.

"Can't have that happening," Nathan agreed. Wiggling his long fingers, he closed in on the girls.

Squealing, they released their hold on Logan and fled toward the open door of the church.

Carter lowered Mason to the ground. "Head on inside, son, and tell your momma I'm on my way." Once he'd gone, his brother turned to Jack. "Good to see you out and about."

The older man nodded. "Good to be out and about."

"How are you feeling?" Nathan asked as his attention turned to the older man.

"Getting my strength back," he replied. "Thanks to your brother and the good Lord I'm standing here today."

"Hope has to be so relieved to finally have

you home again," Carter said. "I know she's been really worried about you."

"I know she was," he said with a nod. "But my little girl needs to stop her fretting. I'm home and on the mend, yet she's hovering over me every second of the day. You'd think I was still on my deathbed."

Logan understood Hope's need to watch over Jack. He and his brothers had done the same with Katie after she'd come so close to dying in the storm that took her momma. But if Hope continued to smother him, Jack was going to rebel. And doing so could put his health at risk. He'd have to add that to the list of things he needed to talk to Hope about.

"Daddy!"

Their gazes were drawn back to the sidewalk just outside the church where Katie stood, hands cupped around her tiny mouth.

"We're getting ready to sing!" she announced excitedly.

"I believe that's our cue to take our seats," Nathan said with a grin as he started toward his baby girl.

Carter followed.

"Be patient with Hope," Logan advised Jack as they fell in behind the others. "You gave her a real big scare. Gave all of us a scare, for that matter. It's gonna take time for her to relax when it comes to your well-being."

Jack chuckled. "And to think I used to be the one giving you advice."

"I learned from the best," Logan said with a grin as they stepped up onto the cement walkway. Both his daddy, God rest his soul, and Jack had been positive influences on Logan's life, making him want to follow their lead in life and be a good Christian who was both honest and hardworking.

"You've learned well, son," Jack said as they stepped into the church. "I'm right proud to see the man you've become."

"Appreciate that, Jack." Now if he could just get Hope to take notice of the man he had become.

Hope fought the surge of tears that threatened to fall as she put distance between herself and the reality of why she'd ended things with Logan. Watching him with his nieces and nephew, seeing the love in his eyes as he playfully teased them. Then she recalled Lily's innocent observation about him needing some little ones of his own. *Maybe someday, sweet pea,* he'd told her.

It had been too much. She'd had to get out of there.

How funny that in a desperate attempt to distance herself from the sight of Logan with his nieces and nephew, children who adored him, she had fled to the one place she never thought she would ever be again—the church she had grown up in.

It had been so long since she'd entered a house of the Lord. But both the sorrow and the dread that filled her before stepping through the wide, open oak doors quickly slid away. She was immediately greeted by people she'd known all her life. Verna, Autumn, Ellie, the reverend's wife, the Parkers and so many more. Most were people she hadn't seen since moving away.

When the reverend's wife made her way over to the church organ, Hope knew it was nearly time for that morning's service to begin. Turning, she scanned the pews, looking for an empty seat for herself and her daddy, and Logan if need be, seeing as how they'd all come together.

Audra and Alyssa waved her over from where they sat near the back of the church. The children had returned from greeting their uncle and were seated next to them.

Hope felt immediately comforted by the women's warm, welcoming smiles and started in their direction. Sliding into the pew they were seated in, she sidestepped her way over to them.

"Morning," she greeted as the two women stood.

"Morning," Audra chirped happily. "It's so good to see you again." She leaned in to give Hope a hug, her rounded belly making it a bit more of a challenge. She laughed softly as she pulled away. "I can't wait to be able to hug people without feeling like I have a beach ball strapped to my stomach."

Alyssa laughed softly. "You're not that big." She leaned past her future sister-in-law to give Hope a quick hug and then added with a grin, "But she should be with as much as she eats."

"I'm eating for two," Audra said in her own defense. "And this is a Cooper I'm carrying inside me."

"That's all the explanation we need," Hope told her, laughing softly. "Those boys have always had bottomless pits for stomachs."

The women nodded in agreement.

"Did you come by yourself?" Audra asked.

"She's here with Uncle Logan," Katie announced with a toothy grin from where she sat with her cousins at the far end of the pew.

Audra turned back to Hope, curiosity lighting her eyes.

"I'm not here with Logan," she said uneasily. "Well, I suppose I am because he brought Daddy and me here, but I'm not *with* Logan."

"I see," Audra replied.

Alyssa nodded in understanding, as well, and then glanced past Audra and Hope, her mouth pulling up into a smile. "I think the boys have returned."

Hope glanced behind her. Sure enough, Nathan and Carter had entered the worship hall and were headed their way. She turned back to Alyssa. "You can see them?"

"Not clearly," she admitted. "But their size gives them away every time. I just don't always know which brother is coming toward me."

She couldn't imagine losing the perfect sight she had always taken for granted. Nodding, Hope moved to let the men into the pew. Once they had taken their places beside Audra and Alyssa, Hope sank down onto the smooth, oak bench and scooted in to make room for her daddy and Logan.

When Reverend Johns's wife began to play the organ, Hope glanced back to find her daddy and Logan moving in quickened strides toward the pew where she sat waiting for them. Instead of her daddy taking a seat beside her, he motioned for Logan to slide in ahead of him, telling him he'd prefer the aisle seat so he could prop his bad arm up on the pew's armrest.

Casting a smile down at her, Logan happily settled onto the pew beside Hope. A few seconds later the music stopped and Sunday service began.

When it ended, Hope was filled with a myriad of emotions. She wanted to be angry with God for taking so much from her, yet sitting there in church that morning, feeling the strong faith of all those around her, had her questioning so many of the choices she had made in her life. While the Lord had called her momma home far too soon, God had given her back her daddy. For that, she was eternally grateful.

And, as hard as it was to accept, it was possible Logan was never meant to be a part of her future, only an emotional stepping stone that would lead her to the life she was meant to live. Yet that life, if this was the future that awaited her, was so empty. She couldn't help but long for what Audra and Alyssa had found with Logan's brothers.

Everyone filed outside the church and then milled about, conversing on the walkway. Hope and her daddy stood waiting for Logan, who had gone around to the back of the church to say goodbye to his family. She wished Autumn was there to talk to while she waited, but her friend had needed to rush off after that morning's services to show a house she had listed in the next town. Hope's gaze drifted in the direction Logan had gone off in. How much longer would he be? Not that her daddy was in any hurry to go. He was content to spend the time talking and laughing with Verna.

The crowd soon began to thin out as that morning's churchgoers headed home, or into town for Sunday brunch. Reverend Johns walked over to where she stood waiting. "I'm glad to have caught you before you and your daddy left."

"We're waiting on Logan. He's around back saying goodbye to his family."

"It was so nice to see you in church this morning."

"It's been a while," she admitted.

He looked toward her daddy. "How's he doing?"

"I think he's pushing himself too hard too soon," she told him. "But Daddy was determined to come this morning."

He nodded in understanding. "I can't imagine much of anything keeps Jack Dillan from attending church. How are you holding up? This can't have been easy for you."

He had no idea. "No, it hasn't been. But I'm feeling a little calmer now that I know Daddy's finally on the mend."

"Will you be staying on?"

"Only until he's cleared to drive. Probably three weeks or so. I need to be here to take him to his physical therapy appointments."

"And to church," he added with unconcealed delight.

Reverend Johns had been the town's preacher for as long as she could remember. He had sat with her many times after church when she was younger, praying with her whenever Hope had needed him to, something she'd done quite often when her momma was sick. She'd needed to know God would hear her prayers and knew that sending her heartfelt message to the Lord through a man of the cloth was a surefire way to make that happen. While her prayers hadn't saved her momma, they had given her a feeling of peace at the time. A peace she hadn't felt since.

Her attention drifted over to where her daddy was laughing aloud over something Verna had just said. His mood had done a one-eighty since leaving the hospital, a good bit of that turn-around no doubt due to the woman standing beside him. But he wasn't completely out of the water yet, and knowing that kept her in a constant state of worry for him.

"Something troubling you?" the reverend asked in that same kind voice she remembered from her youth.

Her focus shifted back to the older man, her first instinct being to tell him that everything was fine. Just as she did with everyone else, keeping her pain and her secrets locked away inside her. But this was a man of the cloth. She couldn't bring herself to give him half-truths. "I worry about Daddy."

"From what I understand, he's doing quite well."

"He is," she agreed. "But I was wondering if you might keep him in your daily prayers for a spell longer."

He nodded. "I can do that. Would you like to share a moment of prayer with me right now? We can thank the Lord for touching your daddy with His healing hands."

"I don't think I can," she said, the admission weighing heavily on her heart. "The Lord and I have...well, we've sort of parted ways."

"I see," the reverend said, his expression impassive. "Would you like to talk about it?"

Did she? Would he understand her reasons for shutting the Lord out of her life? "I'll think on it," she told him, a part of her wanting to open up and confide in someone instead of carrying her burdens alone. Just as Reverend Johns had preached about that morning. His words that day had really struck home.

"I pray you do," he told her. "And, just so you know, the Lord hasn't forsaken you. He will be there waiting with open arms when you're finally ready to return to His flock."

Would she ever be ready to return to her

faith? "Thank you," she said, grateful he hadn't judged her, or tried to push her when she wasn't ready to be pushed. "I'll keep that in mind."

He glanced toward the church as his wife stepped outside, her gaze scanning the few remaining church-goers outside. He gave her a wave.

She waved back with a bright smile.

"I'd best go lock up. I promised Rachel I'd take her out for Sunday brunch today."

"We should be going, too," Hope replied. "I don't want Daddy overdoing things."

"I hope you'll consider taking me up on my offer. If not, I hope to at least see you here with your daddy next Sunday. I think it does him good to have you there with him again."

She nodded and then watched as the reverend walked over to join his wife. It had done her good, too. As hard as that was to admit. With no sign of Logan yet, she set off around the church to find him and tell him they really needed to get going.

The sight she came upon had the tension leaving her as she fought to suppress her laughter. All three Cooper brothers were hanging from the monkey bars by one arm, legs bent to keep their booted feet from touching the bedding of mulch below. And they were making chimpanzee sounds!

The children had fallen into a fit of giggles as they watched the grown men's silly antics.

Hope made her way over to Audra and Alyssa who stood off to the side, shaking their heads and smiling at the men's antics. "They never grow up, do they?" she said, grinning herself.

"Never," Audra agreed.

"And in their Sunday best," Alyssa said, clucking her tongue.

Catching sight of her, Logan straightened his legs until his boots rested on the ground and then released his grasp on the crossbar he'd been holding on to. Grinning, he walked over to Hope and reached for her hand. "Come on, little darlin'."

"Where are…" Her words trailed off as he led her to the swings, the children excitedly following behind. "Logan, what are you doing?"

"Getting you to relax and have a little fun," he replied as he turned her to settle her onto the swing.

"Don't you think we're a little too old to be doing this?" she said as he stepped around behind her.

"Never too old," he answered with a chuckle. His large hands curled around the chains, drawing her back until her beige heels dangled in the air below her. "Now admit you wanna swing," he told her as he held her there. "And no fibbing. I know better."

"Logan!" she squealed.

"I'm waiting..."

"Yes," she blurted out, laughing as her grip tightened around the thick chains beside her. "I wanna swing!"

"Thought so," he said with a husky chuckle as he released his hold on the swing. As soon as she swung back toward him, he sent her forward again.

Katie and Lily raced over to jump onto the two empty swings.

"Push us, too, Uncle Logan!" Katie called out.

"I got them," Mason said as he moved to stand behind his little sister. After giving her swing a push, he did the same with Katie's.

"Appears we've got us a couple of sitters," Carter announced with a grin as he and Nathan joined the other women.

Nathan nodded. "Maybe we can work lunch into the deal."

"Only if Hope and I can spoil them rotten and take them out for ice-cream sundaes," Logan called back as he gave Hope's swing another firm push.

"Ice cream!" Mason hollered. "Yeah!"

"Yummy!" Lily chimed in with a smile.

"Before lunch?" Carter said, sounding a little uneasy about his brother's plan.

"After lunch," Logan told him and then looked to the children. "How does pizza sound? Followed by ice-cream sundaes, of course."

Excited cheers went up from the children.

"Pizza and ice cream?" Carter repeated with a shake of his head. "Reckon I'm not surprised. You've never been one for eating a nutritiously balanced meal."

"How is that not nutritious?" Logan asked. "Throw a few strawberries onto their sundaes and between that and the pizza we'll have all five basic food groups covered."

"I might just have to go with Logan instead," Audra said, running a hand over her swollen belly. "Junior here is doing flips at the mere mention of pizza and ice cream. Maybe even pizza topped with ice cream."

"Eeew!" Katie shrieked.

"Mom," Mason groaned.

Lily looked to her new daddy. "Can I get ice-cream pizza, too?"

Alyssa laughed. "Lily, sweetie, your momma's only teasing about eating the two together."

"I wouldn't be so sure about that," Carter said with a grin. "You should see some of the cravings my wife's had since she's been carrying this little one."

Audra glanced his way. "All women crave dill pickles when they're pregnant."

He raised a dark brow. "Garlic dills to be exact—with chocolate milk."

That got a round of "eews" from everyone, except for Hope. She had fallen silent, struggling to hide her emotions as the conversation turned to Audra's pregnancy.

"Can we go with Uncle Logan and Miss Dillan?" Katie pleaded, her gaze fixed on her daddy.

Lily looked over at Hope, who was swinging beside her. "Please, Miss Dillan. I really love ice cream."

"I do, too," Hope replied, trying to keep the melancholy she felt from showing in her voice. "But I need to take my daddy home."

"He can go with us," Logan suggested.

"Not the best food for him to be eating right now. Besides, he usually doesn't eat lunch until one o'clock or so."

"We can take him home for you if you wanna grab lunch with Logan and the kids," Carter offered. "We pass right by your place on our way home."

Lily's expression turned even more hopeful.

Logan brought Hope's swing to a gentle stop. "We won't be gone long. But if you're not comfortable leaving your daddy, I can run you both home and go back for the kids."

Now all three children were looking over at her, anxiously awaiting her reply.

How was she supposed to say no to those sweet little faces? She couldn't. That was all there was to it. "I think I can get away for a little bit," she told them with a smile. Then she looked to Carter. "That is, if you don't mind giving Daddy a ride home. I made some chicken salad last night. He can have some of that if he gets hungry before I get back."

"We don't mind," he said. "But I was only jesting about us having ourselves a couple of sitters."

"He's right," Audra said, more serious now. "I don't want you to think we make a habit of pawning our children off on others."

"I didn't think that for a moment," Hope assured her. "I really enjoyed spending time with the children the night you had me over for dinner."

"They enjoyed spending time with you, as well," Alyssa said.

"Then I reckon it's settled," Nathan announced as he turned to Audra and Alyssa. "Where would you ladies like to go for our all-adult lunch?"

Audra snorted. "All-adult might be stretching it a bit."

Nathan cast a questioning glance her way.

Her teasing smile widened all the more. "Two adults, myself and Alyssa, and two overgrown 'boys' would be more appropriate. That is, if we're judging by your silly antics a few minutes ago."

Alyssa nodded in agreement. "She has a point."

"I'm hungry," Lily complained with a pout from her perch on the swing, drawing everyone's gazes her way.

"Me, too," Katie agreed with a nod.

"Can we go now?" Mason asked impatiently as he looked up at Logan.

Hope pushed out of her swing, saying to Logan, "I'm ready if you are. I just need to go tell Daddy what the plans are."

"Then let's get this show on the road," he replied, scooping up Lily and Katie as the group started back around to the front of the church.

Alyssa walked next to Hope. "How much longer will you be in Braxton?"

"A few more weeks."

"Good. I was hoping you'd still be here for the wedding. Nathan and I already sent out invitations before we knew you'd be home, but we would really like to add you to our guest list. Your daddy should have the invitation with all the information."

A wedding, one Logan would be attending, was one of the last places she wanted to be at. Even if her daddy accompanied her to it. There would be too many reminders of what she'd almost had. But Alyssa was looking at her with the same hopeful expression the children had written across their little faces back at the swings. Once again, Hope found herself unable to say no to something guaranteed to cause her a good bit of heartache.

Chapter Nine

Hope looked up from the tomato she'd been slicing. The knock at the front door sounded again. Setting the knife down, she reached for a paper towel and quickly wiped her hands. Then she went to see who it was.

Opening the door, she broke into a smile. "Autumn!"

"I should've called first," her friend said fretfully.

"Since when have you known us to ask folks to call before coming to visit?" Hope told her, hoping to ease some of her friend's worry. Autumn seemed a little on edge and she couldn't help but wonder why.

Stepping aside, she said, "Come on in." Between her daddy getting home and Autumn having to leave town for a spell they hadn't had a chance to really spend any time together since that day in Autumn's office. More than anything, she wanted the opportunity to rebuild their friendship.

Autumn stepped inside, looking around. "Exactly as I remembered."

"Daddy's never been one for change," she said, and then recalled his newly laid out plans to travel, even go camping. Maybe he wasn't so against change after all.

"I was hoping you might be able to join me for lunch today," her friend said.

Hope sighed, disappointment filling her. "I'd love to, but I'm helping Logan at the nursery. I just came up to the house to fix Daddy some lunch and then I need to get back."

"Her daddy can fix himself his own lunch," Jack announced behind her as he came down the stairs. "Afternoon, Autumn."

"Mr. Dillan," she greeted. "I'm glad to see you're still up and about."

"I intend to keep it that way," he replied. "I've had more than my fill of lying around in a hospital bed and being smothered by everyone's well-meaning intentions." He looked to Hope. "And Logan's more than capable of handling things at the nursery while you take a little time for a meal with a friend."

"I sliced up a tomato, but I haven't started on your sandwich yet."

"Doesn't take two arms to spread some tuna salad and slap a slice of tomato onto some bread. You go on with Autumn. The two of you probably have a lot of catching up to do. I'll give Logan a call to let him know."

"Thank you, Mr. Dillan," Autumn said, sounding more than grateful for his insistence that Hope take the time to join her. "Your daughter and I really do have a lot to talk about before the miles separate us again."

"Well, then," he said, "you two best run along."

"Call me if you need anything," Hope said as she leaned forward to press a kiss to his cheek. Then she turned back to Autumn. "Do you want me to drive?"

"I asked you to lunch," she said, her smile slightly more relaxed. "I'll drive."

"Have fun, girls," her daddy called back over his shoulder as he made his way into the kitchen.

Hope turned to her friend. "Just give me a second to grab my purse."

"I'll wait for you outside. I need to return a call before we go."

With a nod, Hope went to her room. Not wanting to rush Autumn with her call, she paused to run a brush through her hair, pulling it back into a loose knot at the back of her head. Then she added a dab of pale peach gloss to her lips. Hoping she had given her friend enough time, she reached for her purse and made her way out to the porch where Autumn stood waiting for her.

"Ready?" her friend asked, that semi-frown she'd worn on her face when she'd arrived back in place.

"Ready." Her gaze went to the bright yellow Mustang GT parked in the drive. "Nice car," she said, admiring the sporty car as they walked out to it. "I guess some dreams do come true." Besides the goal she'd had to have her own business someday, Autumn had always talked about having a Mustang when she grew up.

"And some don't," Autumn replied as she slid in behind the wheel.

Something told Hope her friend wasn't referring to Hope's failed dreams with Logan. "Is everything okay?" she asked as she settled herself into the passenger seat.

"It will be," Autumn assured her as she started the car. She glanced Hope's way. "I'm really glad you could join me for lunch today."

"Me, too."

"I ran into Verna in town this morning and she said to remind you that if you need any help where your daddy's concerned just give her a call."

"That's sweet of her."

Autumn turned the car around and headed back down the drive. "Not that it's any of my business, but I think Verna has a thing for your daddy."

Hope smiled. "I think so, too. I have to admit it's a little strange thinking about him being interested in someone after so many years spent being a bachelor."

"And how do you feel about your daddy having his head turned by another woman?" her friend asked. "I know it's not something you've ever had to deal with before."

"I honestly think I'm okay with it," she said and she meant it. "Verna is a wonderful, caring woman, and she's been very good to him."

"Her and Logan both," she said. "He has coffee with Jack either in town or here at the nursery several times a week."

Hope couldn't help but feel a little envious of the time Logan got to spend with her daddy while she was hundreds of miles away. "It's good to know the Lord has blessed him with such caring friends."

The words were out before she thought twice about speaking them. Hadn't she, for years, decided not to give the Lord credit where blessings were concerned since He chose to dole them out only when the mood struck?

But ever since attending her old church again, Hope felt herself having fewer moments of resentment that centered around the things God had taken from her. Her mother, her ability to have children and, as a result of that, her dreams where a future between her and Logan were concerned.

"It's nice to know he'll have her looking after him when I go back to San Diego. I just wish he'd take Reverend Johns's sermon last Sunday more to heart and open up to me about his feelings for Verna."

The sermon that morning had been, of all things, about not carrying one's burdens alone. As if God had been speaking directly to her through the reverend's words.

"I'm sure it's a big step for your daddy, but he should trust you to understand and be happy for him," Autumn said. "Maybe he hasn't quite accepted it himself. Sounds like the two of you need to have a heart-to-heart."

"I agree," Hope replied. "But he's still recovering from the stroke. The last thing I wanna do is add any sort of stress to his life by bringing up something he clearly doesn't feel comfortable enough sharing with me."

"Unless you're against his courting Verna, there shouldn't be any stress involved in bringing the subject up."

Maybe her friend was right. "I want him to be happy. That's all that matters."

"Then tell him that."

Hope smiled. "I think I will."

"I know we were gonna grab a bite in town, but how would you feel about picking up a couple of sandwiches and some drinks and taking them to the park for lunch? It's a beautiful afternoon and it would be a good place for us to catch up without any interruption."

"I'd like nothing more. I spent so much time sitting inside the hospital with Daddy, and now working at the nursery, some time spent outside doing nothing more than relaxing with a friend sounds wonderful."

They drove into town where they picked up lunch and then made their way to the park. Several other townsfolk had decided to take advantage of the pleasant day, spending the afternoon feeding the ducks at the pond or enjoying a casual stroll along the walking path.

The two open-sided picnic pavilions a short distance from the pond were at that moment unoccupied, so Hope and Autumn headed that way, bagged lunches and bottles of chilled water in hand.

"I've been doing a lot of thinking about Sunday's sermon," Autumn said as they settled onto the table benches across from each other.

Hope looked up at her, unsure of where her friend was going with her comment. "It was a good service."

"I know we all have burdens," Autumn began. "Some bigger than others, like the one I've been carrying around for quite some while. A secret that's about to completely change my perfectly laid out life."

At first, Hope thought Autumn was trying to get her to open up. But now, well, she had to wonder if this burden, this soon-to-be drastic change she had referred to, was responsible for her friend being out of sorts that afternoon. "It sounds serious."

"You have no idea," Autumn said, a slight catch in her voice. "I really need to talk to somebody about it." She glanced in Hope's direction. "Someone I trust. And I thought of you."

It touched her deeply that Autumn still thought of her as a friend she could trust with anything. Just as they had when they were growing up. "Anytime you need a shoulder to lean on, I'll be there for you," she told her, meaning it with all her heart. "I'm only a phone call away."

"I wish I had tried to contact you before," she admitted as she peeled open the wrapper of her ham-and-cheddar sandwich.

"You should have," Hope told her as she unwrapped the turkey-and-Swiss-on-wheat sandwich she'd decided to go with.

"You have no idea how many times I picked up the phone to call your daddy to get your number and then hung up, telling myself that this wasn't your burden to bear."

She understood more than Autumn knew about having a burden that weighed heavy on one's heart. "I'm here now."

"I'm leaving Braxton after Nathan and Alyssa's wedding," her friend said as she picked at her sandwich.

Hope's eyes widened. That was only weeks away. "Leaving? As in for good?"

"For as long as it takes."

Concern filled her as she took in Autumn's words. How could her friend just up and leave town? She had a business she'd built there. A life. "Takes to do what?" Hope asked worriedly.

"To help my sister. Summer recently lost her job and has been desperately trying to find another one."

This was about Summer? "Autumn, why doesn't she come home and work with you like the two of you talked about doing when we were younger?"

"I've offered to bring her into the business, but she turned me down. Said she didn't wanna have folks saying they're not surprised she ended up in such a tangle."

Summer had always been known as the wild one, while Autumn had been the safe and predictable one. "She could work at the nursery. I know Daddy and Logan are talking about hiring someone on to help run the place."

"There would be talk if she came home," Autumn said. "Summer doesn't want her daughter to be judged by her momma's past."

Hope nearly choked on the bite of sandwich she'd just taken. After taking several quick swallows of water, she said, "Her daughter? Summer has a child?"

She nodded with a tender smile. "She's almost three. Her name is Blue Belle, but we call her Blue. She's the most precious little girl you could ever imagine. I fly up to Wyoming to see them every couple of months, although most folks think I'm away on business. Every time I see Blue, she steals more and more of my heart."

"I can only imagine," Hope said, stunned by her friend's revelation. "And Blue's daddy?"

"Out of the picture."

"I'm sorry to hear that." Poor Summer.

"It was a rodeo romance that didn't work out," Autumn explained.

Unlike her twin, Summer had always had a

passion for horses and barrel racing, more often than not competing in local rodeos during her teen years. Hope's heart went out to the little girl who would never know the kind of father's love Hope had known from her own daddy. "Summer's blessed to have you to help her out with her daughter."

Autumn's eyes misted over. "I love them both so much. I would do anything to ensure their happiness, even if that means leaving what I've built here and starting over."

"I understand," Hope said, tears welling up in her own eyes. Hadn't she done the very same thing herself? Sacrificed her own happiness to ensure the happiness of someone she loved.

"Hope, are you okay?"

"No," she said with a sob and then shocked herself by blurting out, "I told Logan I didn't love him because I can't have children."

Autumn gasped. "What?"

"That's the burden I've been carrying since I went away to college." She went on to tearfully explain the diagnosis she'd been given and the risks of trying to conceive and carry to term.

Autumn was on her feet and racing around the table to wrap her arms around Hope. "So much makes sense now." She gave Hope a comforting squeeze. "I wish I would've known."

"It wouldn't have changed anything," she told her.

"It would've if I could've talked you into telling Logan the truth. He loved you. Would've stood by you no matter what."

"I loved him," Hope said with another soft sob. "Still do."

"Then take Revered Johns's advice to heart and ease the burden you've been carrying around for so long. Tell Logan the truth."

Panicked, Hope pushed away. "I can't. Promise me you won't, either. I want him to have the family he's always dreamed of having and I can never be the woman to give that to him," she said, tears rolling down her cheeks.

"This breaks my heart because I know how much you love him," Autumn said sadly. "But I give you my word not to tell him. Only please promise to let me share your burdens from now on, so you're not taking them on all alone."

Hope nodded with a sniffle. "Same goes for you."

Autumn smiled. "I'm so glad to have you back in my life again."

While it hurt to revisit the past, there was something about opening up to her friend that was surprisingly cleansing. She no longer had to shoulder the emotional burden she'd taken upon herself alone.

* * *

Her thoughts on the conversation she'd had with Autumn the day before, Hope set another flat of Majestic Giant pansies, one of the nursery's best sellers, onto a display table in front of the greenhouse that housed a large selection of flowers.

It had been so good to talk to her friend. To be able to open up about some of the pain she'd kept lock away inside her for so long. And while nothing had really changed where she and Logan were concerned, she felt a little less troubled by the thought of being around him. A good thing, seeing as they were spending so much time with each other while her daddy recovered.

Humming softly, she made her way along the flat-laden tables. Trays of petunias in varied shades of purple and others in deep, solid pinks filled one side. Across the row, snapdragons stretched upward in vibrant shades of pink, red, purple, yellow, orange and white.

People had already begun their spring planting, so she had been working steady, between checking in on her daddy, to keep a good selection of flowers on display out front.

With all the empty spots on the display tables now filled, Hope stepped back to survey her efforts. A vehicle coming up the drive had her hurrying to wipe her hands on her jeans as she turned to offer a smile of welcome to the arriving customer. Only it wasn't a customer. It was Logan and he was driving a horse trailer.

She watched as he parked his truck and stepped down from the cab, wondering what he was doing there in the middle of the afternoon. Lifting a hand to shield her eyes from the bright rays of the afternoon sun, she called out to him, "Where did that come from?" she said, looking past him to the horse trailer.

"I borrowed it."

"To get more mulch?" she asked, knowing he'd been doing landscaping that week for a nursing home over in the next county.

"To make a delivery for your daddy," he replied as his long-legged strides closed the distance off between them.

"What kind of delivery?" she asked, noting the serious expression he wore as he approached her.

"For an order Jack took."

"Daddy's selling horses now?" she said, wanting to bring a smile to Logan's far-too-serious face.

"A nursery order," he replied with a slight quirk of his lips.

Whatever could a horse trailer have to do

with a nursery order? "First of all," she said, "aren't you working a job today?"

"I was," he said. "But only half a day so I could take care of this issue."

"What issue?"

"The one I've been wanting to talk to you about, but couldn't seeing as how you've taken to avoiding me again," he replied, his searching blue eyes watching for her reaction to his words.

Unfortunately for her, there was no keeping the guilt from her face. He was right. Ever since they'd taken his nieces and nephew out for lunch and ice cream the week before, she'd been trying to avoid spending time alone with Logan.

It was getting harder and harder to fight her feelings for him. Being with him felt good. It made her happy, genuinely happy. At the same time, seeing him with Katie, Mason and Lily that day and the smile of pure joy they brought to his face had been a stark reminder of what Logan longed for. Children of his own.

"I saw you last evening," she countered. Logan had stopped by to check on her daddy after work that day and to ask if anything needed done at the nursery before he went home for the night.

"Do you really want me discussing issues that I've needed to take care of in regards to the nursery in front of your daddy?" He sighed. "On second thought, I probably should be doing just that. It is Jack's business."

Her gaze locked with his. "Issues?"

Logan nodded. "I've taken care of most of them, but I think you should be aware of where things sit."

"Most of them?" she gasped.

"There have been a few things that have come up since Jack was in the hospital. This particular issue has to be seen to first thing tomorrow morning. I'm only telling you this now because I didn't want you wondering why there was a horse trailer parked here."

"Why am I only hearing about there being problems now?" she asked, angry that he had kept the truth from her. "And don't say it was because I was avoiding you. Because when Daddy first came home from the hospital I wasn't. Not until I had such a good time with you and the children at Ryan's place." Despite her anger, her tone held a measure of hurt, as well.

He folded his muscular arms across his chest and raised a dark brow. "You've been avoiding me because you had fun the day we took the kids out for pizza and ice cream?"

Had she said that? Recalling her frustrated outburst, she concluded that she had indeed let that slip. Frowning, she said, "Don't try to change the subject, Logan Cooper. You and I were supposed to be working together to keep the nursery going. How is your having kept things from me considered working together?"

He sighed. "I tried to talk to you the day you came home to get the house ready for Jack's release from the hospital, but you were preoccupied. Understandably so," he added. "And since you've brought your daddy home you've been running yourself ragged in your efforts to take care of both him and Hope's Garden. So I made the decision to handle things on my own."

She couldn't deny that she had been doing just that. If only she had known the talk he'd wanted to have with her that day he'd stopped by to check on her was about issues with the nursery, she would have stopped cleaning out the fridge long enough to hear him out. But she'd assumed he'd wanted to discuss where things stood between them personally, something she wasn't emotionally prepared to address at that point.

"You shouldn't have made the decision for me," she told him.

"Maybe not," he agreed. "But I did what I did because, foolish or not, I still care about you. And I care about Jack. My handling this matter was meant to take the burden off both your shoulders."

There was that word again—*burden*. First in

Reverend Johns's sermon and then from Autumn and now Logan. Was this the Lord's way of making her rethink the way she had chosen to live her life? Of letting her know she truly didn't have to carry her burdens alone?

I still care about you. Logan's admission made her want to jump for joy, and at the same time weep. She'd missed him so very much. But she couldn't give in to her own needs. It would be a mistake. "Logan..."

"Hear me out, little darlin'," he insisted, meeting her panicked gaze. "I really thought I'd finally managed to push you from my heart. Felt secure in the fact that you could never hurt me again. But I was wrong. There is no pushing you from my heart, Hope, because you are my heart."

She gasped softly, tears filling her eyes. "Don't say that."

"Just speaking the truth."

She turned away so he wouldn't see the tears of regret in her eyes. She was going to hurt him again and she felt helpless to stop it.

Firm hands closed over the tops of her shoulders, gently turning her. Logan, with his deep, heart-melting blue eyes stared down at her. "I've missed you."

"I've missed you, too," she heard herself say.

"Glad to hear it," he said before lowering his mouth to hers in a tender kiss.

She knew she ought to push him away, remind him that she would be leaving Braxton soon and that he needed to direct his heart elsewhere. But Hope couldn't bring herself to do what needed to be done. Instead, she accepted his kiss, cherished it, wanting to hold on to the memory of it once she went back to San Diego.

Logan ended the kiss, stepping away with a wide, knowing grin. "I've waited what feels like forever to hear you say those words."

"Logan," she groaned. "We're getting sidetracked." She turned to the long wooden display table behind her where she stood fussing over the flats of flowers, straightening them with her now trembling hands. "What exactly have you been keeping from me?"

Logan made no more mention of the kiss they had just shared. Instead, he went on to tell her about finding order sheets lying atop a shelf inside one of the greenhouses instead of in the office where Jack always kept them.

She pivoted to face him. "So the horse trailer really is for a nursery order?"

He nodded. "It's a loaner from Billy Denton. I needed to borrow it to make a delivery to Merlington tomorrow morning."

Hope's Garden didn't offer deliveries. Logan knew that. "Why are we delivering an order to

Merlington? Or anywhere, for that matter. We don't do that here."

His expression turned serious. "I didn't have a choice."

And then she understood. "Daddy agreed to it?"

"I don't think he meant to. But the receipt was marked for delivery instead of pickup, an easy enough mistake since the boxes are next to each other on the order sheet."

"But he's been filling out those sheets forever," she said with a troubled sigh, and then shook her head. "I don't know why I'm questioning this. I know Daddy wasn't thinking clearly in the weeks before his stroke with his blood pressure so dangerously high. I found the overlooked utility bills to prove it."

"There were unpaid utility bills, too?"

She stopped and turned to look at him. "Too?"

Logan nodded. "There were a couple of supplier accounts that hadn't gotten paid."

"Oh, no," she groaned. "How much? I have money in my savings I can use until I make sure Daddy's checkbook is accurate. The last thing I wanna do is start bouncing checks."

"I've already paid them off."

Her head snapped around, her gaze locking with his. "What do you mean *you've* paid them off?"

"I used my own money to settle those accounts." He stood and rounded the desk.

"Logan, no," she breathed.

"It's gonna be okay," Logan assured her with a tender smile.

Hope tilted her head to look up at him. "How much?" she demanded. "I'll write you a check. I just need to transfer the funds from my savings to my checking account."

"I'm not taking your money, Hope," he said. "Jack will pay me back when he's able to. Just as I did the money he loaned me."

"What are you talking about?"

"Forget I said anything," he muttered. "I didn't mean to bring my and Jack's past business arrangement into this conversation. What I'm trying to say is that I know your daddy's good for the money."

"I'm sorry," she apologized. "I didn't mean to pry. Your financial troubles are none of my business."

"There were no financial troubles," he said. "Jack loaned me money to start my landscaping business. Put his faith and his trust in me right from the start, and I've worked very hard to make certain your daddy never regretted believing in me."

"I had no idea," she said softly.

"You wouldn't," he told her. "I asked that this

be kept between Jack and me. A man has his pride, you know. But I've long since paid him back. That doesn't mean I'm no longer in his debt. I owe him so much."

"You saved his life," she told him. "That's more than enough. Getting back to this Merlington delivery. What are we delivering that requires a horse trailer to get it there instead of Daddy's pickup?"

"The mall in Merlington is getting an internal makeover. They're expecting eighteen large-leaf potted plants for the inside corridors."

"Eighteen!" she gasped, panic assailing her. *Oh, Daddy.* "We don't have that many to give them."

"We do now," he calmly assured her. "They're gonna get what they ordered."

She looked up, meeting his gaze. "But how?"

"I made a few calls and found a nursery in Coopersville that has the seven additional plants we need to complete the order. They're holding them for pickup first thing tomorrow morning. We'll lose a little profit doing it this way, but it's better than losing a customer. And Billy Denton is lending me his trailer free of charge."

She stepped forward, throwing her arms around him. "Logan, you're a lifesaver." The second she realized what she was doing, she pushed away in a fluster. "Sorry. I didn't mean to…"

"Little darlin'," he drawled, cupping her chin tenderly as he smiled down at her, "it's all right."

All right would be her not having practically squeezed the stuffing out of him in her excitement. All right would be her not having let him kiss her a few moments before. As far as she was concerned, nothing was all right.

"You might wanna hold your opinion of my abilities to yourself until after this job is completed to everyone's satisfaction," Logan said with one of those adorable, slightly crooked Cooper grins that never failed to make her feel as though butterflies had just taken flight inside her belly.

He let his hand drop back down to his side. "I'll be leaving for the delivery around seven thirty tomorrow morning, but I'll be here earlier than that to get the trailer hitched back up to my truck."

"We will," she corrected.

His brow lifted. "We?"

"You're not making the delivery alone. I'm going with you tomorrow."

"There's no need," he countered. "I've worked the delivery into my regular landscaping schedule."

"There's every need," she said determinedly. "This is my family's business. I should be the one taking responsibility for my daddy's unintentional actions. Not you."

"Have you ever driven a truck that's pulling a horse trailer behind it?" he asked.

"No. But there's always a first time," she countered with a determined smile.

"Look," he said, "I offered to help Jack out until he's back in the saddle. So at least part of the responsibility rests on my shoulders."

Very broad shoulders, she thought admiringly. "Then there's no argument," she pointed out. "Daddy's counting on both of us to keep things running smooth at the nursery. That means we do this together."

He nodded. "I'm fine with that. But what about Jack? Don't you think he's gonna wonder where you've gone off if he decides to take a walk down to the office and you're not there?"

"I didn't consider that." She pursed her lips in thought. There was no way around it. Her daddy was going to have to know about this delivery, because leaving Logan to handle it all by himself wasn't right.

"I'll talk to Daddy tonight and tell him about the mix-up with this order. Unless he asks, I'm not bringing up any of the other issues. I just hope he doesn't take a mind to do any sort of work at the nursery while you and I are away."

"We shouldn't be gone that long," he assured her. "If Jack wants to hang out in his office and answer phones, nothing more, that would be okay. And it would give him something to do other than sit around up at the house. I know he's been going stir-crazy."

"What if a customer shows up before we get back?" she asked worriedly.

"Your daddy's plenty capable of handling things here for the short time we'll be gone," he assured her. "The nursery doesn't even open until ten. And most folks tend to stop by the nursery during the afternoon hours. But just to be safe, we'll leave the Closed sign up at the entrance off the main road."

"You've thought of everything," she told him. He had a way of making things in life sound so uncomplicated when it was anything but.

"Hope," he said, gaining her attention, "It's all gonna work out just fine. You're just gonna have to trust me."

Trust was never something she had an issue with when it came to Logan. "You seem to have everything under control. I'm not sure I would have even known where to start."

"With or without me," he told her with a smile, "you would've figured it out."

"I'm glad I don't have to find out. And for the record," she added with a tender smile, "I do trust you." It was her heart she was worried about. She couldn't give in to the love she felt for him, because he deserved to have the same happiness his brothers had found. A life that included the children she could never give him.

Chapter Ten

She trusted him. Those words Hope had spoken the day before had meant the world to Logan. Trust was very important in a relationship, and so was honesty. Now he needed to be completely honest with Hope.

"Morning."

He glanced up from Jack's desk where he'd been finishing up the paperwork they would need for that morning's delivery. A slow smile slid across his face. "Morning."

Hope stepped into the office. "I just came from talking to Daddy."

"Everything okay?" he asked, trying to read her mood.

"He was upset that his mistake would be putting you out, but when I told him I was gonna make the delivery with you he settled down."

"Reckon he figured it was a good thing I'd

have someone along to see to the heavy lifting," he teased, wanting to see that smile that followed him into his dreams.

It worked. "If only I were an ant," she said with a feigned sigh. "Then I'd be able to lift twenty times my weight. But as it stands, I don't think I'll be much help."

"Got it covered," he said with a grin and then turned back to gather up the paperwork. "I loaded a couple of four-wheel dollies onto the trailer. Moving the plants into the mall won't be an issue."

He turned from Jack's desk to find Hope looking up at the framed picture of herself with her daddy and her momma that hung on the office wall. She couldn't have been more than four or five at the time. Her momma had Hope propped up on one of her hips, a joyous smile lighting both of their faces as Jack stood next to them, arm draped lovingly around his wife's slender shoulders.

Sensing a change in Hope, Logan moved to stand beside her. "Your daddy treasures that picture."

"I know," she said, a hint of melancholy to her voice. "I can still remember that day. Daddy brought Momma home a couple of rosebushes and we helped her to plant them in the garden in front of the house. Deep pink roses, because they were her favorite and she was so happy. Your momma and daddy stopped by to see them and took a picture of us standing next to Momma's garden. She loved her garden."

"And what about you, Hope?" he asked. "What do you love?"

She turned to look at him. "Excuse me?"

"What makes you smile like your momma was smiling that day?" he asked, wanting to know. Wanting to be the one who put a smile on her face.

She shrugged her reply. "I don't know."

"You should," he said. "You deserve someone special in your life making you smile."

"How do you know there isn't someone special in my life?" she said a little too defensively.

"Because I know you, and you would never have kissed me back yesterday if there had been someone special in your life right now."

"You sound so sure of that," she said with a challenging glance.

"I'm sure of you," he told her.

"Maybe you're wrong about me. Maybe I've changed."

He chuckled. "We've all changed, Hope. But deep down you're still that same girl I fell in love with. That goodness is too ingrained in you for it to be otherwise."

"There isn't anyone special in my life," she

admitted, much to his surprise. "Hasn't been anyone…since you."

Logan's heart slammed against his chest. A myriad of questions flitted through his mind. Was that because a part of her still loved him? Was it because she was afraid of someone doing to her what she'd done to him? Or had Hope given up on love the way she'd given up on her faith? Whatever the reason, it was hers to give explanation to or not. He couldn't force it.

"Same here," he said with a nod.

"You've dated," she stated knowingly.

"Checking up on me, Hope?" he teased.

"More a case of word getting around in this small town," she said in explanation.

He nodded. Not much got past the town grapevine. "While we're being completely honest with each other," he said, "you asked me once why I was doing this. Helping your daddy out and all."

"I remember."

"Well, it goes without saying that I'd do it to help Jack out because he's a good friend. But truth is I'm doing whatever I can to make it easier for him because I feel responsible for his taking ill."

She looked up at him in confusion. "Why would you feel responsible for what happened? Daddy had a stroke because he stopped taking his medication. You had nothing to do with that."

"Maybe not, but if I had paid better attention I might have seen some sort of warning sign that something was off." Concern dragged the corners of his mouth downward. "Looking back, I realize now that Jack wasn't his usual self before the stroke. Only I wrote it off to his just being distracted with nursery matters. I should've known it was something more."

"If I had been living here, making sure he kept up on all of his medications, he might not have had that stroke," she countered. "Should I blame myself for his taking ill? Because, believe me, the thought has crossed my mind so many times since coming home I've lost count."

"No," he said without hesitation, looking down into those caring green eyes. "You don't live here. But I do. I'm closer to Jack than anyone here in town. I can't help but blame myself for allowing this to happen."

Hope reached up, resting her hand on his cheek. "Daddy doesn't blame you, Logan. And neither do I."

He brought his hand up to cover hers, giving it a gentle squeeze, and for a long moment their gazes locked and held. It felt like old times. Back when they were both young and in love.

"Hope…" Before he could voice what he was feeling, she pulled away.

"While we're laying things out on the table so to speak, we need to talk about the offer Daddy made you."

"I haven't accepted," he told her.

"I know. Daddy mentioned that you were having some reservations because of me."

"Of course I'm having reservations, Hope. This is your family's nursery. You should be the one to take over the running of it."

"I can't," she said, her expression before she looked away pained.

"Can't or won't?" he heard himself saying.

She didn't answer.

"I'm sorry," he said with a sigh. "That was uncalled for."

"I want you to accept his offer to become his partner," she said, her gaze fixed on the happy family looking back at her through the thin layer of glass.

"I'm not sure how I'd work it out," he admitted, wanting to be honest. "I have my own business to run, and Jack sounds like he wants to step away and become more of a silent partner."

"I can't think of a better business merge," she told him. "You could run your business out of the nursery. Hire someone on to work here while you tend to your landscaping jobs. You'd get your trees and plants and flowers at even more of a discounted rate. And someday it'll be your family picture hanging in a frame on this wall."

"Hope…"

She turned to face him, tears in her eyes. "I mean it, Logan. I'm okay with this. You know the business inside and out and Daddy trusts you implicitly. I can go back to San Diego knowing that Hope's Garden is in good hands."

Panic surged through him. He didn't want to hear her talk about leaving. Didn't want to hear about his future family's picture hanging on that wall. Unless she was part of that happy family. But to make that happen he needed more time with her outside of working together at the nursery.

She wanted him to do this. Of that, he had no doubt. And she was right. Landscaping and nurseries pretty much went hand in hand. Jack had taught him how to run a nursery from the ground up, so that wouldn't be an issue. He could find a way to make it work. Would find a way. For Jack and for Hope.

Logan nodded. "I promise to give it some serious consideration."

"Thank you," she said, the relief clear in her voice.

"Reckon we best get a move on," he told her,

more determined than ever to convince her to stay.

Plants loaded into the horse trailer, they climbed into Logan's pickup and headed out on their delivery. Billowy, white clouds filled the morning sky. "Thankfully, it looks like it's going to be a beautiful day," Logan noted.

"Enjoy it while it lasts," she told him. "The weather station is predicting possible thunderstorms later this evening."

"Crazy spring weather. Beautiful one minute, rainy the next." He glanced her way. "Tell me about San Diego."

Hope looked to him in surprise before finally replying, "There's really not much to tell."

"You've lived there since graduating from college," he reminded her. "Surely, there's something that stands out in your mind about the town you live in."

"It's big," she said, her head turning away as her gaze shifted to the passenger window and the passing scenery outside.

"Bigger than Braxton," he said. "That's for sure."

"Too big," she murmured quietly, but he hadn't missed her uttered remark.

"So what do you do for fun in your 'too big' town?"

"I work."

She worked. He took a moment to mull that over in his mind. A necessity, of course, but not exactly fun in the sense he'd been referring to. "So your job keeps you pretty busy," he deduced from her reply. Was that why she wasn't in a relationship?

"Do we have to talk about me?" she said without so much as a glance his way.

"Just trying to make conversation," he replied, wondering why she found it so hard to answer such basic questions about her life. "Would you rather talk about me?" he teased.

That got her attention. Looking his way, she said, "Yes."

"I'm an open book, little darlin'," he said as they pulled out onto the main highway. "But before you start throwing questions my way, there's one more thing I need to know. You still like to dance?"

She hesitated before nodding. "Yes."

"Good. Because I wanna dance with you, Hope. Be my date for the wedding."

His date? "Logan." She sighed. "I don't think—"

"Don't give me your answer yet. Sleep on it tonight and then let me know. Now it's your turn. Ask away."

"Why aren't you married?" she blurted out

and then gasped as if horrified the question had come out of her mouth.

"Reckon I haven't found the right woman yet," he said, not wanting to get into all the reasons why he hadn't. Because his heart had been broken when she'd ended things. His trust in love had been shaken. Because no other woman had ever made him feel the way she once had. Still did, if he was being completely honest with himself.

"What about Autumn?" she said.

His head snapped around. "Autumn?"

Hope bit at her bottom lip as she gave a shake of her head. "Never mind. That wouldn't work. She's gonna…I mean she travels too much. What about Lizzie? She's pretty and sweet and loves children."

His gaze returned to the road. "Autumn is a friend, but like I said—not the right woman. Lizzie," he said with a chuckle, "is a great girl. Not my type, either. Not to mention my best friend is crazy about her."

She gasped. "He is?"

"Yep. Only Ryan hasn't quite figured that out yet," he explained.

"Well, then, what is your type?"

He looked her way with a grin. "You."

"Logan…"

"Logan me all you like, little darlin', but I'm a

man on a mission." A mission to win her heart, to be exact. And the good Lord willing, that was exactly what he intended to do. Because he felt it more than ever in his gut that Hope wasn't happy in San Diego. More important, she wasn't happy with some other man. She was free to woo, and woo her he would.

Hope glanced out the kitchen window, taking in the first rays of morning light as the sun began its ascent into the big blue Texas sky. Dew clung to the grass and coated the leaves, its tiny, crystal drops glistening like scattered diamonds under the sunlight. Her gaze moved beyond the yard and the trees to the distant hills that she and Logan had once taken long hikes through. God-given beauty one saw so much less of in a big city.

You still like to dance? Logan's words had played over and over in her mind all night.

Yes, she'd answered. Though she couldn't recall the last time she had done so. But she hadn't forgotten all the dances she'd gone to with him when they were young. Or how special it had felt to be held in his loving arms as he whirled her around the dance floor.

I wanna dance with you, Hope, Logan had said. *Be my date for the wedding.*

"A penny for your thoughts."

Startled, Hope turned to find her daddy standing in the kitchen doorway. "Daddy," she said, "you're up early."

"You're up earlier," he countered with a smile. "What has you looking so pensive this morning?"

"A lot of things," she answered with a sigh.

A warm smile moved across his face. "Care to share?"

"I was just thinking about how much I miss looking around me and seeing hills and trees and wide expanses of land still untouched by man."

He nodded in understanding. "There is something about waking up to God's beauty every morning."

Instead of to the world of concrete she had made her home in.

"You said everything went okay with the delivery yesterday," her daddy went on. "Was that the truth of it? I don't want you holding things back from me."

"Yesterday's delivery went off without a hitch," she assured him, feeling guilty that they had kept some things from him. But his health was more important to her than hurting his feelings. "In fact, they said we can expect more business from them in the future."

"If everything went well, why are you standing here staring out the kitchen window at the crack of dawn?"

"I couldn't sleep," she said with a reassuring smile.

"And there's gotta be a reason for that. I know it's not because you're still worrying yourself over me. I'm feeling great. My therapy is going well. Look what your old daddy can do now," he told her. Then, raising his weak arm, he curled it up to make a muscle. The movement was slow and thought out and a little shaky, but definitely progress in the right direction. "I'll be ready to dance with Verna by the wedding," he added excitedly.

"You like her," she said softly.

Her daddy chuckled. "Who doesn't like Verna?"

"I'm not referring to that kind of liking her," Hope clarified. "You have a tender spot for her in your heart. What I wanna know is what's keeping you from acting on it?"

Her daddy looked unsure of what to say.

"If you're worried about hurting me by opening your heart up again, don't even give it a second thought," she told him. "I think Verna is a wonderful, kind and giving woman. And I know it wouldn't change the way you felt about Momma."

"It's a big step," he muttered uneasily. "And I'm feeling like a newborn colt. Not so steady on my legs where that kind of relationship is concerned."

"The first step is the hardest," she told him. "But I think it's time you take it. You're too special of a person to spend the rest of your life alone."

"I could say the same thing about you," he said, emotion making his voice catch. "I love you, honey."

"I love you, too, Daddy," she said, stepping forward to give him a hug.

"Logan's a good man," he said when the hug ended. "To think that you're standing here giving me advice about having a tender spot for someone and not acting on it. I've seen the way the two of you are around each other."

"It won't work," she told him, doing her best to hide the pain of knowing that caused her. "Not in the long run. But Logan is the reason I couldn't sleep. Not that I don't always have your welfare in my thoughts."

"So what has you chasing your tail where that young man's concerned? His partnering with me to run the nursery?"

Her gaze snapped back up to meet her daddy's. "He accepted?" Not that she should be surprised. She had given him her blessing.

He nodded with a smile. "Called last night to let me know. He's gonna stop by this week so we can sit down and hammer out the details. We just have to fit a time in that's good for the both of us. Between his landscaping jobs, the nursery and my therapy, time is limited. Now getting back to Logan being the reason you were up before the rooster crowed..."

She might as well tell him. He'd find out sooner or later anyway. "He asked me to go to Nathan and Alyssa's wedding with him."

"Sounds like a nice gesture if you ask me. Not something to lose sleep over, mind you."

She sighed tiredly. "It is nice. But I don't wanna give him the wrong idea. I'll be leaving Braxton in a couple more weeks."

"Don't remind me," he muttered not-so-happily.

"Daddy, I have a job I need to get back to."

"Reckon so," he conceded. "Guess I should be thankful that I've had you here as long as I have this time. And that the Lord saw fit to bring you and Logan together long enough for the two of you to be able to mend your fences."

Of course he was thankful she and Logan were able to be in the same room with each other. Her daddy had never given up on her and Logan getting back together, no matter how many times she'd told him it would never happen.

Maybe if she told him the truth, he'd stop pushing for things to be more than they could be. And if the Lord did have something to do with bringing her and Logan together to smooth the waters between them, then for that she was eternally grateful.

At least now she could return to Braxton for a visit and not feel the need to avoid Logan. As if that would even be possible now with Logan taking over part ownership of the nursery. The hard part was seeing him, knowing that he still cared about her, and not giving in to her heart's yearning to tell him her true feelings. Despite Reverend Johns's sermon, some burdens were just better off carried alone.

"If you're still mulling over your decision, I think you should accept Logan's invitation," her daddy told her, bringing Hope back to the conversation they'd been having. "Attending a wedding with someone doesn't mean the two of you will be next in line. Go. Have fun. Live it up a little. You're too serious these days."

"Live it up a little," she repeated with a smile. "Never thought I'd hear my daddy giving me that piece of advice."

"Advice we both need to take to heart," he said with a chuckle. Then his expression grew serious. "You know, every night in that hospital I prayed to the Lord to heal me, promising not to take my life for granted anymore. A person starts taking not only his or her life for granted, but their faith, as well. I intend to work less and play more, appreciate even the smallest of things that touch my life, and maybe even live it up a little myself at the wedding."

Maybe he was right. What harm would there be? From the sound of things, her daddy intended to. She had to wonder if she even remembered how to have fun. Then she recalled the water hose battle she'd gotten into with Logan and smiled. She'd let loose that day and it had been fun and freeing. For the first time in years, she'd felt alive.

"I see I got those wheels inside your pretty little head a-turning," her daddy teased.

Hope laughed. "They're a bit rusty, but they are definitely turning. I'm gonna accept Logan's invitation, but not without making certain he has no further expectations where he and I are concerned. And then I'm gonna go to that wedding and kick up my heels."

"That's my girl," her daddy said, his smile widening into a toothy grin.

"You know, Daddy. With Logan helping to run the business, you'll be able to come to California to visit me. You might even have time to take that camping trip you talked about in the hospital," she added with a grin.

"Maybe I'll come to California to visit *and*

take you camping with me somewhere near you."

"I'd like that," she said with a smile. "But one of us had better learn how to set up a tent before that happens."

"Won't need to," he said. "I told you I wanna buy myself a camper. And that's what I intend to do. I'm too old to be sleeping on the hard ground."

She looked at him. "You're really serious about this, aren't you?"

He nodded, happy grin widening. "I wanna make the most out of every minute the good Lord has given me. As soon as my therapist gives me the green light, I'll be doing a little traveling. But first, I'm gonna get the chance to enjoy life with a sweet little Texas rose at Nathan's wedding. Make sure to do the same with Logan." That said, her daddy left the kitchen, whistling happily.

Could she do it? Really enjoy herself? It wasn't as if Logan was taking her to a movie. They would be going to a wedding. A joyous occasion for Nathan and Alyssa, even young Katie. But it was going to be a bittersweet occasion for her, Hope thought regretfully. Sitting beside Logan as they listened to the vows being spoken, vows they had once thought they would be sharing with each other, dancing with him—as friends—when she had never stopped dreaming about more, would be one of the hardest things she ever had to do.

Maybe a few hours of tending to plants at the nursery would help to ease the anxiety she was feeling. Grabbing up her purse, Hope slipped out the back door and started down the drive. Noticing Logan's truck parked in the lot, her heart quickened. He wasn't there to work. He had come for her answer.

She rounded the building, her gaze sweeping the front grounds of the nursery, but Logan was nowhere in sight. She went in search of him, finally locating him behind one of the greenhouses, hard at work. He was busily stacking the bags of shredded hardwood bark mulch that had been delivered to the nursery the afternoon before.

The sleeves of his jean shirt had been rolled up to his elbows. He'd removed his cowboy hat, hanging it atop a nearby fence post. And he was whistling a happy tune. So like the Logan she remembered.

Logan glanced up from the bag of mulch he was reaching for to see Hope standing there, a bright smile gracing her pretty face. His own mouth quirked into a happy grin. "Morning."

She moved to stand beside him, her gaze

shifting to the neatly stacked mulch bag. "Morning. I didn't expect to see you here."

His grin widened. "Didn't you? You told me you'd give me your answer today."

"I meant this evening when you stopped by after work."

"I have a couple of hours before I'm scheduled to arrive at my landscaping job today, so I thought I'd swing by. Truth is, I wouldn't be worth much if I spent the day distracted, wondering what your answer was gonna be."

"Before I do, we need to set some ground rules," she said, biting at her bottom lip.

He nodded obligingly. "Set away, little darlin'."

"If I go to the wedding with you, it's as friends."

"Not so sure that rule is necessary," he told her. "We are friends."

"You know what I mean, Logan Cooper. No kissing me," she said, a soft blush moving over her face.

"Are you allowed to kiss me?"

"Logan…"

"I think it's a fair question," he said.

"It's an unnecessary question," she told him. "All we'll be doing is dancing. Can you accept that?"

"Let's see," he said, pretending to mull things

over. "Going to my brother's wedding with some-one I really enjoy spending time with. Getting to hold her in my arms while we dance the night away. Yep. I can live with that." *For now.*

She smiled. "Then I accept your invitation."

Logan said a silent prayer of thanks to the Lord for bringing Hope back into his life. "I'm real glad." Reaching out, he plucked his cow-boy hat off the fence post and dropped it onto his head. "I'll pick you and your daddy up on Saturday around four thirty."

"That sounds good. But it might only be me," she said with a knowing smile.

He looked at her questioningly.

"Let's just say I have a feeling that when Daddy finds out I've got a date for the wed-ding he's gonna bow out of going with me and ask Verna to go with him instead. He's already commandeered half of her dance card."

He studied her for a moment before asking, "Are you okay with that?"

"More than okay," she said. "Daddy and I talked this morning. I want him to be happy. He's been alone for so very long. I told him that I think it's time for him to open up his heart to loving someone again."

"Sounds like good advice," Logan replied. Now, if he could just get Hope to heed her own words. "Before I go, I also wanted to let you know that I've decided to accept Jack's offer."

"I know," she said with a grateful smile. "Daddy told me this morning. I know it means a lot to him to have you coming on as a partner, even taking over completely once he's ready to step away from the nursery for good."

"It would mean more to him to have you be a part of it."

"He understands, and you're like the son he never had," she told him. "Who better to take over? I'll admit it's gonna be hard to see Daddy step away from something that's been such a huge part of his life for so many years. But knowing that you'll be the one taking over is surprisingly comforting to me."

"It's gonna take a little juggling things around on my part to make it all work, but I've given it a lot of thought and it feels right."

"It is right."

"Well, I appreciate the trust Jack's willing to put in me and I'm gonna make certain he never has any reason to question his decision to bring me into the business."

"Daddy's not the only one who has faith in you."

"That means a lot, little darlin'." He pulled his truck keys from the front pocket of his jeans. "Now that I've got my answer, the one I'd been hoping for, I'll be on my way. Have a good day. I know I will."

He walked away whistling a happy tune, his heart feeling lighter than it had in years.

Chapter Eleven

"Sugar," Jack Dillan called up the stairs, "your ride's here!"

Hope's stomach flip-flopped. She cast a panicked glance toward the oval oak floor mirror that had once been her momma's. Audra and Alyssa had taken her to the mall in Coopersville to find a dress for the wedding. She wanted something new to wear for this special night, even if nothing more would come of it than a night out with a "friend."

The dress she'd chosen was a deep emerald green with short fluttery sleeves and a tea-length, whispery skirt. A belt of the same chiffon material tied in a soft, rather simple bow on one side of her waist. Her heels were a pewter color that matched almost perfectly the clutch purse she had found to go with her dress.

She'd pulled her hair up into a clip with several loose, curling strands framing her face. Her makeup consisted of mascara with a hint of dark brown eyeliner on her upper lid, a sweep of bronzer on her cheeks and a soft pink lip gloss. For someone who normally went only with mascara and a clear lip gloss, this was a huge change. But Alyssa and Audra had talked her into purchasing the blush and the eyeliner, and she had to admit it made her green eyes stand out.

A tap at the bedroom door had her turning from the mirror just as her daddy poked his head into the room. "Everything okay, sugar?"

She took a deep, calming breath before replying, "Why wouldn't it be?" Other than she'd waited forever for this night. For the chance to be with Logan again while life's realities took a step back.

Tonight she wasn't the woman who had cut herself off from her past, hurting people that she loved more than anything. Tonight she was a woman determined to enjoy every second of the time spent with Logan, laughing, smiling, feeling alive.

Her daddy's gaze moved over her. "You look beautiful, honey."

Hope glanced down at her dress. "It's not too much? Audra said it suited my coloring."

He chuckled. "Sugar, I'm not the man whose

approval you're seeking, but I will say that you're every bit as perfect as the first bloom on a rosebush."

Tears sprang to her eyes. "It shouldn't matter."

"But it does," he said knowingly. "If it makes you feel any better, Logan is pacing the entryway as we speak, leaving a trail of aftershave behind him."

Surprise lit her face. "Aftershave?" Logan never wore aftershave, always saying women were put on this earth to smell pretty, not men.

Her daddy nodded. "Reckon he's looking to impress someone this evening."

Exactly what she didn't want to happen and yet, at the same time, a ripple of excitement moved through her.

"Best get yourself downstairs," he said with a warm smile.

Hope reached for the pewter clutch, took a deep breath and then started for the door, her daddy right behind her. "Is Verna here yet?"

"Not yet," he replied. "Can't say that I like having my date pick me up."

"It's only until you're cleared to drive," she told him as they made their way down the hall to the stairs. "That'll be here before you know it."

Her daddy's nearness seemed to give her the

courage she so desperately needed at that moment. Logan's approval shouldn't matter to her, but it did. More than it ought to, all things considered.

Halfway down the carpeted steps, Hope heard Logan's sharp intake of breath. Her gaze met his as he moved to stand at the base of the stairs.

"You look beautiful," he said, the sentiment so clearly heartfelt she had to struggle to keep the tears at bay.

"Thank you." She took in the sight of him, as well, dressed in black pants and a charcoal-gray, long-sleeve shirt. The black tie he'd chosen had a subtle diamond pattern the same shade of green as her dress. It was as if they'd done so intentionally. "So do you," she said distractedly.

"That's what I was going for," he said, a grin lighting his tanned face. "Beautiful."

It took a moment for his words to settle in, and then warmth seeped into her blush-tinged cheeks. "I meant handsome," she corrected with a nervous smile. This didn't feel like a date between friends. It felt like much, much more. A beginning where there couldn't be one. An emotional pulling when she ought to be pushing away.

Logan held out his hand.

Placing her much smaller hand in his, she let him assist her down the last step to the landing below. Memories of town dances Logan had picked her up for, church socials and their senior prom came rushing back.

She'd been so happy back then. And despite all the stress she'd been dealing with in regards to her daddy's health and the issues with the nursery, she felt happy now as Logan stood looking down at her the way he once had when they were young and in love.

When she left Braxton, most likely in the next week or so, she would remember this night fondly.

A horn beeped outside.

"That'll be my ride," her daddy announced, his face beaming with happiness.

"We should get going, too," Hope said anxiously. The sooner they were at the church, mingling with the other wedding guests, the better. Less chance of her thoughts remaining solely on Logan Cooper and that heart-melting, slightly crooked grin of his.

Logan nodded. "This is one wedding I can't be late for. I'd never hear the end of it."

They stepped out onto the porch with her daddy just as Verna was coming up the steps. She looked positively glowing in a champagne-colored chiffon skirt and matching jacket. Her hair had been done in an updo that left a few spiraling strands against the sides of her face. A pair of pearl earrings completed the lovely ensemble.

"You didn't have to come to the door," her daddy said with a stubborn lift of his chin.

Hope looked to him in surprise. What kind of greeting was that?

Verna looked to Hope's daddy. "I know it's been a while since either of us has gone out on a date, but not so long I don't remember that it's a show of respect to greet your date at their door when picking them up."

"But you're a female," her daddy replied as if aghast at the thought.

Logan attempted to smother his snort of laughter as he stood beside Hope. Then he bent to whisper near her ear, "He's done it now."

"Glad you finally noticed," Verna responded with a delighted smile.

Hope was pretty sure her daddy had noticed a long time ago, but hadn't been quite sure what to do about it.

Verna didn't give Jack a chance to respond. Instead, she stepped up beside him, slipping her arm through his. "I'll help you to the car and you can tell me how fetching I look as we walk."

"It's my arm that's healing, not my leg," Hope heard her daddy grumble as Verna Simms led him away. "But you do look fetching."

Hope stood watching them go, happiness for her daddy filling her. "She's good for him," she said with a soft sigh.

* * *

Logan nodded in agreement. Verna was good for Jack. Just as he wanted to be "good" for Hope. The way she had looked at him when she'd come down the stairs to greet him said more than words ever could. Words she stubbornly refused to speak.

Hope still cared about him—deeply. He'd felt it more and more over the past several weeks she'd been back in Braxton, but for some reason she was determined to keep those feelings locked away.

Offering her the crook of his arm, Logan walked Hope out to his truck. "We could've all driven to the wedding together," he said as he slid behind the wheel and started the engine.

"I think Daddy wanted to spend a little alone time with Verna, because I suggested all of us riding to the wedding together and he gave me some excuse about the older folk probably not staying as late as us young folk would."

"If I know Verna, she'll probably be the last one off the dance floor," he said with a chuckle as they pulled away from the house. "That woman's got more energy than all of us Cooper brothers combined."

That had Hope frowning. "I hope Daddy doesn't overdo things tonight."

Logan glanced her way. "Have you seen the

way Verna mothers your daddy? She'll have him seated comfortably by the dance floor, glass of sweet tea in hand, while she joins the gaggle of females that always gather together to do those group line dances."

"I've seen men join in those dances, too."

"Not this man," he said without hesitation. "Carter probably. Nathan for sure because it's his wedding and it wouldn't do for him not to join in. Myself, I'll be seated next to your daddy, sipping at my own glass of sweet tea."

"So you wouldn't join in if I asked you to dance with me?"

His mouth quirked up into a crooked grin. "Reckon we'll just have to find out."

A little over an hour later the ceremony was over and Logan found himself standing next to Hope out on the dance floor at his brother and Alyssa's reception. They were attempting to learn some sort of dance that called for a lot of fancy footwork, but his focus kept drifting back to the wedding ceremony. He longed to exchange those same vows, those same promises of love with Hope. He wanted to build a life together with her.

"For not wanting to join in on the group dances, you're sure picking up the steps quickly," Hope said as she rose up to whisper near his ear. "In fact, you're keeping up with Mrs. Cross quite nicely."

He snorted, drawing several curious looks their way. Thankfully, it was time for the group to turn, which put him and Hope in the back row and everyone's attention directed elsewhere. Leaning over, he whispered back, "Mrs. Cross is ninety-two years old."

She shrugged. "Just imagine how good you'll be in sixty-five years." Laughing softly, Hope stepped away as the group shifted once again.

It was so good hearing her laughter. It was the most relaxed he'd seen her since she'd come home. Although the water hose fight had come close.

Things felt right between them. Like the nine years of heartache had never happened. She had even allowed him to take hold of her hand as they left the wedding ceremony at the church and walked to the reception, which was being held in the town's newly built recreation center.

But he wanted more than to hold her hand. He wanted to hold her heart.

Logan caught Nathan's grin from across the dance floor. Just as he'd told Hope, his brother was out there with his beautiful new bride, struggling every bit as much as his little brother was to stay in step with the gaggle of sure-footed females. His brother's gaze shifted to Hope, whose smile was lighting up the room, and then back to Logan. Nathan nodded, giving his unspoken approval of Logan bringing Hope back into his life, into their lives.

"I think Ryan's had a change of heart," Hope said when the dance ended and Logan moved to escort her off the dance floor.

He followed the direction of her gaze to see his best friend cozying up to Lizzie Parker over by the lemonade table. They were actually smiling at each other. "It's about time," he muttered, happy for his friend.

"Must be something in the air," Hope said, pointing toward the dance floor.

Logan looked to see Jack and Verna having that slow dance she had promised him. His friend couldn't seem to take his eyes off the woman in his arms. Love seemed to be in the air for more than just the bride and groom. It was all around him. Right beside him, in fact, Logan thought as his attention returned to his date for that evening. There was no doubt in his mind that he loved Hope. Had never really stopped loving her.

When the night ended they said their goodbyes to his family and then walked back to the church where Logan had left his truck. "Thank you for making me dance," he said, grinning down at Hope.

Her expression softened as she looked up at him. "Thank you for putting yourself out there."

She hadn't seen anything yet. But he needed to bide his time. "I think Jack had a good time tonight," he said as he helped her up into the truck's cab.

"I hope so," she said, a hint of worry coming over her face. "He seemed a bit quiet toward the end of the evening. And they left early. You don't think it had anything to do with Verna, do you? I mean, Daddy is a little rusty where dating is concerned."

Jack and Verna had left the reception a little over an hour before, but they'd seemed happy, if not a little tired from all the trips they'd made out onto the dance floor. "I'm sure he was just taking a moment to take it all in," he assured her. "He's been mostly cooped up since his stroke."

"I hadn't thought about that," she said, her worried expression easing.

He closed the door and rounded the truck, sliding in behind the wheel. "And I don't think you need to worry about him and Verna leaving the reception a little early. I'm thinking they wanted to spend a little quiet time together before the night ended."

That made Hope smile. "Maybe Daddy isn't

as rusty at romance and dating as I thought him to be."

Logan chuckled. "It's like riding a bike." Only with Hope it was like riding in the Tour de France with all of its ups and downs, needing to know when to hold back and when to push harder. Tonight he would definitely be pushing.

By the time they arrived back at Hope's place, Logan's heart was thrumming in his chest. He prayed to the Lord to give him the courage to do what his heart was leading him to do.

"The lights are on," Hope noted. "Daddy must have waited up for me."

Logan nodded.

"I hope the night ended well between Daddy and Verna."

"I'm sure it did," he told her as he walked her to the front door. "Speaking of night's ending, I hate to see this one end for us."

"We knew it had to," she said softly.

"But does it?"

Hope looked his way. "What?"

"This doesn't have to be the end of things," he said, his heart pounding even more. "It could be a whole new start."

"Logan..." she groaned. "We agreed. Tonight was about us being friends."

"What if I tell you I want more?" he said, hopeful. "All those things we dreamed about having years ago. A life together. A house filled with children."

She looked away, falling silent.

He could feel her pulling away and refused to lose her yet again. "The good Lord brought us back together for a reason. I'd like to believe it was because *we* were meant to be. Don't let this chance we've been given slip away. Let's put the pain of the past behind us and look to the future."

"I can't," she said, her voice quivering. A phrase Logan had heard from her before. "If Daddy's doctor clears him to drive next week, I'll be heading back to San Diego." Her gaze dropped to the weathered porch floor between them. "That's where my future lies."

Her words stung, but he was a Cooper. Stubborn as the day was long. He wasn't giving up without a fight. Not when he knew she still cared for him. If only he knew what it was that kept her from admitting the truth, even to herself.

"There are plenty of people who have managed long-distance relationships," he said determinedly. "I'm willing to do whatever it takes to make it work between us, little darlin'." He took her hands in his, giving them a gentle squeeze. "I want you in my life again. Tell me you're willing to give us a second chance."

She bit at her bottom lip. Then she lifted her

tear-filled gaze to his and shook her head. "I can't."

"You can't?" he repeated.

A lone tear slid down her cheek. "You deserve a woman who will love you. One who can give you the happiness you deserve."

"You can be that woman, Hope."

"A woman who shares the same unbendable faith as you," she continued, as if not hearing his words. "One who will give you the large family you've always wanted. I will never be that woman," she said with a sob before pulling her hands free of his and disappearing into the house, the screen door slamming shut behind her.

While Hope hadn't spoken the words this time around, he'd still heard them loud and clear— *I don't love you*. Couldn't love him. Turning, Logan walked away, all the joy he'd felt that evening fading away. He'd put his heart on the line and she'd thrown it back into his face—*again*.

He'd only made it halfway down the walkway when Hope screamed his name. There was no mistaking the panic he heard in her voice. Racing back to the house, he flung the door open to find Hope standing at the foot of the stairs, holding her daddy up. Jack's face was pale, his body sagging against his daughter's much slighter form.

Logan moved to take Jack's weight from her,

holding the older man up. "Call 911," he told a sobbing Hope.

"I don't need 911," Jack muttered stubbornly.

"I don't think you're in any condition to argue," Logan told him, nodding to Hope, who dug her cell phone out of her purse with trembling hands.

Thirty minutes later Hope was seated beside Logan in the waiting room of County General. They had yet to hear any news on her daddy's condition.

Hope looked up at Logan, who had driven her there after the ambulance had taken her daddy away, tears streaming down her cheeks. "He came out of the living room to greet me as I was starting up the stairs. The second he saw me crying, he hurried toward me, asking what had happened. Then I saw the color leave his face and he began to sway. And then—" A sob escaped her.

Logan reached for her hand. "It's gonna be okay. No matter what happens, I'm here for you."

Even after pushing him away again, he was still there for her. She'd wanted so badly to say yes when Logan had asked her to give their relationship a second chance. Longed to be a part of his life again, because even after all of these years she had never stopped loving him. But when he'd mentioned the house filled with children, it had broken her.

"Hope?"

She looked up to see Reverend Johns standing in the waiting room doorway.

"I was here looking in on Mr. Wilkins and heard they'd brought your daddy in."

She nodded with a soft sniffle. "They're running tests to see if he's had another stroke."

"I'll keep him in my prayers," the older man replied with an empathetic smile. Then he looked to Logan. "Please keep me updated on Jack's condition."

"I will," Logan said, concern etched on his face.

The reverend turned away, starting for the door.

"Reverend Johns," Hope called after him, her heart pounding.

He turned with a comforting smile. "Yes?"

"Do you think you might be able to stay for a moment longer to pray with me?"

Logan gave her hand a gentle squeeze, the comforting touch saying more than words ever could. Then he stood. "I need to make some calls and say a few prayers of my own."

She watched as he left the room and then looked to the reverend as he took a seat beside her on the vinyl sofa. "Before we say a prayer for Daddy, I need to ask the Lord for His forgiveness." Her prayers would mean nothing if she didn't make amends with God. They needed to be heard. But what if her prayers weren't enough, as they hadn't been for her momma?

Hope pushed her fears aside and turned to the Lord. No matter what happened she knew she needed God back in her life. A feeling of peace came over her as she welcomed Him into her heart.

Then she and Reverend Johns prayed for her daddy.

"Would you like for me to sit with you?" the reverend asked after all of their prayers had been sent heavenward.

Hope shook her head. "Thank you for the offer, but I think I'd like a little time alone to have a few more words with the good Lord."

"I understand." He pushed to his feet and then turned to smile warmly down at her. "Jack's in good hands. Both here on earth and from the Lord above."

"I know," she said softly, tears in her eyes. "Thank you for stopping by."

"Anytime," he replied.

Hope sank back against the sofa cushion. Then closing her eyes, she began to pray.

"Ms. Dillan?"

Her eyes sprang open, her gaze flying to the emergency room doctor she'd been talking to earlier standing in the waiting room entrance. "Yes?" she answered, shooting to her feet.

"We've gotten the test results back and there is no sign of another stroke. This was a medication issue, causing his blood pressure to drop. We'll adjust his meds, get him leveled out and then send him on his way."

Relief swept through her with such intensity, she had to sit down. "So he's gonna be okay?"

"He's already chomping at the bit to get out of here, if that tells you anything," the doctor answered with a grin. "You're welcome to see him now if you'd like."

Hope nodded, tears filling her eyes. "I'd like that very much."

Logan had felt a moment of panic when he'd returned from calling his brothers to find Hope gone. Reverend Johns had passed by him on his way out to the parking lot, so he knew she wasn't with him.

What if she'd gotten word on her daddy and it wasn't good? That would mean she'd been left to face whatever it was all alone.

He turned from the waiting room, moving in hurried strides to the nurses' desk down the hall. Thankfully, the news was good and Hope was, at that moment, seeing her daddy.

Logan was directed to the cubicle where Jack had been placed. When he'd heard Hope's cries that evening, seen Jack struggling to stand, he'd feared the worst. But God had heard his prayers. *Hope's prayers*, he thought with a smile as he neared the room.

"This is what you've been keeping from Logan all these years?" Logan heard Jack say.

Logan stopped in his tracks. Once again, he'd walked in on a conversation he wasn't meant to overhear.

"I shouldn't have said anything," Hope answered, her words catching. She stood alongside Jack's hospital bed, her back to the cubicle's entrance. "But when you started talking about being here for your grandchildren it just came out. There will never be any grandchildren, no matter how much I long to have a child of my own. Children of my own. Not with the severity of my endometriosis."

"Why didn't you say something?" he asked, his own voice taut with emotion.

"I couldn't risk Logan finding out the real reason why I pushed him away," she said with tears in her eyes. "I know him and he would've sacrificed his own happiness to stay with me. I couldn't bear that, Daddy. To think that his love for me kept him from having the family he has always wanted."

"Sugar," Jack said tenderly.

"I love him, Daddy. Enough to let him go. Logan deserves a woman who can give him the family he's always wanted, something I'm not physically able to do. Not without great risk. So, please, let it go."

All of a sudden, everything made sense. Hope's pushing him away all those years ago. Her leaving town. The wistful look in her eyes whenever Audra or the children were near.

I love him. How he had longed to hear those words from her. Nothing else mattered. "What he's always wanted," Logan said as he stepped into the tiny room, "is you."

Hope spun around, teary eyes wide. "Logan," she gasped, the color draining from her face.

"Son," Jack said, a slow grin moving across his face, as if the Calvary had just arrived to save the day.

"Jack," Logan muttered, never taking his gaze from Hope's beautiful face. He closed the distance between them in two long strides and drew her into his arms. "All these years I've wondered how I could've been so wrong about us. About your love for me." He reached out to cup her face. "That's because I wasn't wrong."

She closed her eyes, tears tracking down her

cheeks. "Nothing's changed. We can't be together."

"Oh, little darlin', that's where you're wrong," he told her as he gently brushed her tears away.

"Daddy told us boys there is always hope beyond the storm. Your leaving me was the storm I've been weathering for the past nine years. Your love pushed the rest of those dark clouds away, leaving in its wake a glorious rainbow. *You* are my hope beyond the storm, and this time I'm never gonna let you go."

"I can't give you what you need," she said with a sob.

"If you're referring to children, there are plenty of kids out there needing someone to love them," he told her. "We could have that family we dreamed of having."

"But they wouldn't be yours," she said with a sniffle.

"Not by blood," he agreed. "But family is more than that. It's a blessing from God. It's an opening up of the heart to love without reservation. Just as Carter's done with Audra's children. They aren't blood related, but he loves them as if they were a part of him."

"He does," she said softly.

"Come home, Hope," he said, looking into her eyes. "To me."

"And me," Jack tossed out, drawing both their gazes his way. "Sorry," he said with a sheepish grin. "Go on, son. I think she's softening toward you."

Logan chuckled. "I sure hope so, because I'm about to put my heart on the line. That is, with your blessing, I'm gonna."

Hope gasped.

Jack's grin widened. "Son, you've had my blessing from the first moment you put stars in my baby girl's eyes."

Taking Hope's hand in his, Logan settled onto one knee, smiling up at the woman he loved.

"This wasn't how or where I had envisioned doing this, not even when. I don't even have a ring. But I'm not about to let you run out on me again, Hope Dillan. I love you too deeply. Always have. That's why I never completely stopped holding on to hope."

Her free hand flew to her mouth as she bit back a sob.

Logan smiled warmly, his heart filled with love. "I'm gonna be your daddy's partner in business. Let me be your partner in life. Let me give you all of those things we used to dream about when we were younger, including a house of our own that's overflowing with children. Children we'll adopt and welcome into our hearts, share our faith with, make a happy, loving family with. Tell me you still want those things, Hope."

"I do," she said with a teary nod.

"Then let me give them to you. Marry me. It doesn't have to be tomorrow. Take all the time you need. I just need to know that you have faith in me, in the future we can have together if you choose to give us a chance."

She looked down at their joined hands and then met his searching gaze, her beautiful green eyes filled with emotion. "It's because of the faith that I have in you, and the faith I have found once again in the Lord, that I can say without any doubt—yes."

"Yes?" he repeated, praying he hadn't imagined her response.

"That's what I heard," Jack said, moisture filling his eyes.

Hope laughed softly. "Yes," she repeated with love in her eyes, "I will marry you, Logan Cooper. I can't imagine spending the rest of my life anywhere else but with the man that I love, have always loved, and with whatever children the good Lord sees fit to bring into our lives."

Logan stood and drew her into his arms for a tender, heartfelt kiss.

"Appears we'll be keeping Hope's Garden in the family after all," Jack announced beside them.

Logan pulled away from Hope with a chuckle and then slipped his arm around her waist as they turned to face her daddy. "Appears we will at that."

Epilogue

Hope couldn't help but smile as she stood looking up at the newly framed picture on the wall of the nursery's office. Behind the crystal-clear glass, Hope, Logan and the precious little boys, ages four and six, they had been blessed to adopt and make their own smiled back.

They were surrounded by family. Grandpa Jack and his blushing new bride, Verna Simms Dillan. Uncle Nathan and his growing family—Alyssa having given birth to their second son six months before the family portrait had been taken. Uncle Carter and his growing family, which consisted of three strapping Cooper boys and the ever adorable Lily.

True happiness filled Hope's heart as she looked upon all those she loved and was loved by. Her life had changed so much since moving home to Braxton, and she had God to thank for it.

Despite having shut him out of her life for far too many years, He had forgiven her, welcoming her back into His flock with open arms. He had blessed her with a husband who had seen to it she had the family she had always wanted.

Sons who made her wonder every day how she could have ever thought her future happiness ended with her inability to have children of her own. These two little gifts from God, who had come into their lives for safekeeping, had given her more joy than Hope had ever thought possible. She'd also been given brothers and sisters, nieces and nephews, and even a stepmother whom she adored.

Giggles mixed with the oh-so-familiar husky laughter of her husband filtering in through the open window drew Hope outside in search of her family. Shielding her eyes from the brilliant rays of the afternoon sun, she watched as her sons chased their father around with garden hoses, cold water soaking him clean through.

"How about some help over here, little darlin'?" her husband called out with a grin as he attempted to dodge the two, well-aimed streams of water.

"Looks to me like the boys have got things well in hand," she called back, laughing softly.

"I was referring to me," Logan called out as the boys tackled him with no resistance whatsoever to the ground, smothering him in hugs and kisses.

Hope took a moment to send a silent prayer up to God, thanking Him for sending her down this path He had chosen for her. Then, with a wide smile, she stepped forward, joining in the wonderful madness that was her life.

* * * * *

If you want to find out more about how brothers Nathan and Carter Cooper found love, be sure to pick up the other books in the TEXAS SWEETHEARTS *miniseries from author Kat Brookes:*

HER TEXAS HERO
HIS HOLIDAY MATCHMAKER

Available now from Love Inspired!

Find more great reads at
www.LoveInspired.com

Dear Reader,

I hope you've enjoyed reading Hope and Logan's story in *Their Second Chance Love*. There are times in life we find ourselves traveling on a path we hadn't intended to go down. Times when we set aside our own happiness for the sake of someone we love. Just as Hope felt she was doing when she ended things with Logan. Whether her decision was the right thing to do at the time or not, it was done because she loved Logan so deeply.

We all make sacrifices in our lives for those we love, be it something small that comes with everyday choices, or something much more life-changing. But it's those decisions and seeing them through that make us stronger emotionally and spiritually. It also helps to prepare us for those times in life when we are given a second chance at life and, as in Hope and Logan's case, love.

I'd love to hear what you thought of Hope and Logan's second chance at love. Email me at kat brookes@comcast.net. For news on upcoming releases, check out my website at katbrookes.com, or stop in and visit me on Facebook.

Blessings,
Kat

Get 2 Free Books,
Plus 2 Free Gifts—
just for trying the Reader Service!

YES! Please send me 2 FREE Love Inspired® Suspense novels and my 2 FREE mystery gifts (gifts are worth about $10 retail). After receiving them, if I don't wish to receive any more books, I can return the shipping statement marked "cancel." If I don't cancel, I will receive 4 brand-new novels every month and be billed just $5.24 each for the regular-print edition or $5.74 each for the larger-print edition in the U.S., or $5.74 each for the regular-print edition or $6.24 each for the larger-print edition in Canada. That's a savings of at least 13% off the cover price. It's quite a bargain! Shipping and handling is just 50¢ per book in the U.S. and 75¢ per book in Canada.* I understand that accepting the 2 free books and gifts places me under no obligation to buy anything. I can always return a shipment and cancel at any time. Even if I never buy another book, the 2 free books and gifts are mine to keep forever.

Please check one: ☐ Love Inspired Suspense Regular-Print   ☐ Love Inspired Suspense Larger-Print
(153/353 IDN GLQE)   (107/307 IDN GLQF)

Name	(PLEASE PRINT)

Address	Apt. #

City	State/Prov.	Zip/Postal Code

Signature (if under 18, a parent or guardian must sign)

Mail to the **Reader Service:**
IN U.S.A.: P.O. Box 1867, Buffalo, NY 14240-1867
IN CANADA: P.O. Box 611, Fort Erie, Ontario L2A 9Z9

Want to try two free books from another series?
Call 1-800-873-8635 or visit www.ReaderService.com.

* Terms and prices subject to change without notice. Prices do not include applicable taxes. Sales tax applicable in N.Y. Canadian residents will be charged applicable taxes. Offer not valid in Quebec. This offer is limited to one order per household. Books received may not be as shown. Not valid for current subscribers to Love Inspired Suspense books. All orders subject to credit approval. Credit or debit balances in a customer's account(s) may be offset by any other outstanding balance owed by or to the customer. Please allow 4 to 6 weeks for delivery. Offer available while quantities last.

Your Privacy—The Reader Service is committed to protecting your privacy. Our Privacy Policy is available online at www.ReaderService.com or upon request from the Reader Service.

We make a portion of our mailing list available to reputable third parties that offer products we believe may interest you. If you prefer that we not exchange your name with third parties, or if you wish to clarify or modify your communication preferences, please visit us at www.ReaderService.com/consumerschoice or write to us at Reader Service Preference Service, P.O. Box 9062, Buffalo, NY 14240-9062. Include your complete name and address.

LIS17R

Get 2 Free Books,
Plus 2 Free Gifts—
just for trying the Reader Service!

HARLEQUIN

HEARTWARMING™

YES! Please send me 2 FREE Harlequin® Heartwarming™ Larger-Print novels and my 2 FREE mystery gifts (gifts worth about $10 retail). After receiving them, if I don't wish to receive any more books, I can return the shipping statement marked "cancel." If I don't cancel, I will receive 4 brand-new larger-print novels every month and be billed just $5.49 per book in the U.S. or $6.24 per book in Canada. That's a savings of at least 19% off the cover price. It's quite a bargain! Shipping and handling is just 50¢ per book in the U.S. and 75¢ per book in Canada.* I understand that accepting the 2 free books and gifts places me under no obligation to buy anything. I can always return a shipment and cancel at any time. Even if I never buy another book, the 2 free books and gifts are mine to keep forever.

161/361 IDN GLQL

Name	(PLEASE PRINT)	
Address		Apt. #
City	State/Prov.	Zip/Postal Code

Signature (if under 18, a parent or guardian must sign)

Mail to the **Reader Service:**
IN U.S.A.: P.O. Box 1867, Buffalo, NY 14240-1867
IN CANADA: P.O. Box 611, Fort Erie, Ontario L2A 9Z9

Want to try two free books from another line?
Call 1-800-873-8635 today or visit www.ReaderService.com.

* Terms and prices subject to change without notice. Prices do not include applicable taxes. Sales tax applicable in N.Y. Canadian residents will be charged applicable taxes. Offer not valid in Quebec. This offer is limited to one order per household. Books received may not be as shown. Not valid for current subscribers to Harlequin Heartwarming Larger-Print books. All orders subject to credit approval. Credit or debit balances in a customer's account(s) may be offset by any other outstanding balance owed by or to the customer. Please allow 4 to 6 weeks for delivery. Offer available while quantities last.

Your Privacy—The Reader Service is committed to protecting your privacy. Our Privacy Policy is available online at www.ReaderService.com or upon request from the Reader Service.

We make a portion of our mailing list available to reputable third parties that offer products we believe may interest you. If you prefer that we not exchange your name with third parties, or if you wish to clarify or modify your communication preferences, please visit us at www.ReaderService.com/consumerschoice or write to us at Reader Service Preference Service, P.O. Box 9062, Buffalo, NY 14240-9062. Include your complete name and address.

HWI7

HOMETOWN HEARTS ♥

YES! Please send me **The Hometown Hearts Collection** in Larger Print. This collection begins with 3 FREE books and 2 FREE gifts in the first shipment. Along with my 3 free books, I'll also get the next 4 books from the Hometown Hearts Collection, in LARGER PRINT, which I may either return and owe nothing, or keep for the low price of $4.99 U.S./ $5.89 CDN each plus $2.99 for shipping and handling per shipment*. If I decide to continue, about once a month for 8 months I will get 6 or 7 more books, but will only need to pay for 4. That means 2 or 3 books in every shipment will be FREE! If I decide to keep the entire collection, I'll have paid for only 32 books because 19 books are FREE! I understand that accepting the 3 free books and gifts places me under no obligation to buy anything. I can always return a shipment and cancel at any time. My free books and gifts are mine to keep no matter what I decide.

262 HCN 3432 462 HCN 3432

Name	(PLEASE PRINT)	
Address		Apt. #
City	State/Prov.	Zip/Postal Code

Signature (if under 18, a parent or guardian must sign)

Mail to the **Reader Service:**

IN U.S.A.: P.O. Box 1867, Buffalo, NY. 14240-1867
IN CANADA: P.O. Box 609, Fort Erie, Ontario L2A 5X3

* Terms and prices subject to change without notice. Prices do not include applicable taxes. Sales tax applicable in NY. Canadian residents will be charged applicable taxes. This offer is limited to one order per household. All orders subject to approval. Credit or debit balances in a customer's account(s) may be offset by any other outstanding balance owed by or to the customer. Please allow 4 to 6 weeks for delivery. Offer available while quantities last. Offer not available to Quebec residents.

Your Privacy—The Reader Service is committed to protecting your privacy. Our Privacy Policy is available online at www.ReaderService.com or upon request from the Reader Service.

We make a portion of our mailing list available to reputable third parties that offer products we believe may interest you. If you prefer that we not exchange your name with third parties, or if you wish to clarify or modify your communication preferences, please visit us at www.ReaderService.com/consumerschoice or write to us at Reader Service Preference Service, P.O. Box 9062, Buffalo, NY. 14240-9062. Include your complete name and address.

READERSERVICE.COM

Manage your account online!

- Review your order history
- Manage your payments
- Update your address

We've designed the Reader Service website just for you.

Enjoy all the features!

- Discover new series available to you, and read excerpts from any series.
- Respond to mailings and special monthly offers.
- Browse the Bonus Bucks catalog and online-only exculsives.
- Share your feedback.

Visit us at:

ReaderService.com

RS16R